RIGHT
as
RAYNE

M. J. CARLEY

ISBN 978-1-64670-615-0 (Paperback)
ISBN 978-1-64670-616-7 (Digital)

Covenant Books, Inc.
11661 Hwy 707
Murrells Inlet, SC 29576
www.covenantbooks.com

PROLOGUE

Odessa, Texas
1913

Rayne stood in front of the floor-length mirror in her mother's room. She was not inspired by what she saw staring back at her. Freckles were scattered across her cheeks and slender nose. Her blue eyes were thickly lashed, and her mouth was rather wide and full. She had very curly red hair that hung just below her shoulders. The dress she had been bribed to wear was a high neck, long-sleeved prairie dress in yellow that made her hair look an even brighter shade of red; she was not very happy. Her father, Bob Whitmore, owner of the Circle W ranch, had commanded her ever so nicely that she was to wear the dreaded dress when she accompanied him to town the following day; she was not interested. It had been nine months since she had worn a dress and didn't like being reminded of the day they buried her mother. Rayne tried to decide if she would look better with her hair up or down. She ultimately decided that because she was only eleven and didn't have anyone to impress she would wear it tied back. She pulled her hair back, securing it with a ribbon and stomped downstairs. She knew her father would be at the barn hitching the horses up to the wagon; she might as well go out there instead of sulking in the house.

She went down the front steps, and turning right, she spotted her father with the wagon. Sam, their foreman, was working a young colt in the corral when she walked up. He looked toward her, startled at the transformation from tomboy to young lady. "My, you look different, Ray. Not a bad different, a good different. Very pretty," he said with a wink.

"Well, thank you, Sam. Too bad I don't share your opinion. I feel like a fish out of water! How are you supposed to muck stalls in this getup?" she shot back.

"Well, my guess would be, little lady, that you would not muck stalls at all. Ladies spend their time making doilies and playing the piano," he returned.

"Good thing. I'm not a lady then, huh?" she said and with a huff climbed into the buggy. Her father took his seat beside her. With a slap of the reins, the horses pulled the buggy out of the yard and onto the worn road toward town.

Sam wiped his brow with the back of his hand and decided it would take a team of Clydesdales to pull that girl to charm school. She had a sharp tongue and didn't like to be told how she should behave. After Jane, her mother, had died, it didn't take long for the dresses to come off and the work clothes to go on. She trailed her father all day long and could match the work done by most of the hands on the ranch. She loved the ranch and believed it would be hers one day. Not that that was a bad idea, but a woman would need a man to share the work and her life with. Sam only hoped she could keep her mouth shut long enough to find one that would have her.

As the wagon clanked along, Ray and her father rode in silence. Her father had a grin on his face and still couldn't believe he had actually gotten her to put on the dress. She wasn't happy about it, but she would usually do anything her father asked her. Only she didn't wear it because he asked her to; she wore it because he had finally resorted to bribing her. She would get one silver dollar for accompanying him to town in the dress which Ray would no doubt spend on candies at Baker General Store. She was his only child, and he loved her with all of his heart, but how would she ever find a man to take care of her if she didn't dress pretty to attract them? Now of course she was only eleven, but you have to plan ahead. And even now if you were to ask her if she was going to get married, she would say, "Nope, I'm going to live with my daddy on the ranch forever. Everything will be right as rain." That was her favorite saying. He guessed it was crazy for them to have named her Rayne, but Jane had known she was a free spirit, not able to be tamed or controlled. When they reached town, Bob would go to the bank and make a withdrawal then send Ray on to get her candies while he visited a few friends.

As they rode into town, he saw Jim Hale, owner of the Rocking J ranch, his neighbor whose land bordered his. They shared a pond between their lands, and their families have been bickering over the rights to that water for years. No one would give into the other, so their grandfathers had learned to share. They both watered their cattle there. Jim had a son three years older than Ray. Jackson Hale was very high strung like Ray, but that was expected in a boy who was getting very close to being a man. Ray also could not stand the sight of Jackson or Jake, as everyone called him. Every time those two were within a few feet of each other, they were fighting. Jake could find nothing better to do than to taunt Ray about being a tomboy. *Well, let's just see what he thinks when he sees her in a dress*, Bob thought to himself with a sly grin. He can't very well call her a tomboy in a yellow dress.

As they pulled up in front of the bank, Ray noticed Jim's wagon at the store; she gave a long sigh. Gosh, why does he have to be in town on the one day I wear a dress? She decided she would just ignore him. If she didn't pay any attention to him, then he couldn't cause her trouble, right? She could only pray that was true! Her father handed her a silver dollar, and she made her way across the street to Baker General Store.

Shorty and J. W., both hands from the Rocking J ranch, were standing in the doorway of the store talking. When they noticed Ray walking up the steps, they stopped their conversation and looked at her with wide eyes. "Hi, Ray. You look pretty in that dress. I almost didn't recognize you," Shorty said after an awkward silence. Ray couldn't think for the life of her why they would call a man that seemed as tall as the sky, Shorty. She smiled at them and walked on past. She wasn't surprised that they seemed shocked. She herself was shocked when she put the dress on. It was definitely not a good thing, and she couldn't wait until they were back home, so she could pull this thing off and put her pants and work shirt back on.

Mr. Baker was standing at the candy counter waiting for her when she got inside. "Hi, Mr. Baker. How are you today?" she said in a surprisingly cheery voice, she didn't feel. The older man cleared his throat and smiled at her. "Ray, you sure are very pretty today. Are you celebrating something special?" he asked her.

She replied with genuine cheer, "Why, yes, I am. I got a silver dollar from my daddy for wearing this dress, and I'm going to spend it all on candies!"

Mr. Baker chuckled and gave her a friendly wink while he started bagging up the ones she chose. Mr. Baker got them all bagged up and took her dollar for payment. When he handed her the bag, she gave him another big smile and turned to leave. About that time, Jake started into the store. When he saw her, he instantly froze. His eyes wide and roaming over her mass of red curls tied back with the ribbon and her yellow dress. Obviously, the other boys were still busy in conversation and didn't notice that Jake had stopped. Barreling into him, they shoved Jake forward, and he fell right on top of her. She hit her head on the wood floor just as the candy bag fell out of her hand. The bag fell to the floor beside her and spilled the contents all over the dirty wood floor. Ray took one hard look at Jake as she heard all of his friends laughing at the two of them. Jake jumped up off of her and tried to help her up. She slapped his hand away and, with a huff, ran outside and into the road. She saw her father sitting in the wagon across the street talking to another rancher; she headed straight for the wagon, not looking back. When she reached him, she climbed up and ushered her father to leave. He said his goodbyes and started the horses onto the road back toward their ranch. At the edge of town, she chanced a look back to the store and was instantly angry at the sight on the porch. Jake was standing on the porch with his friends laughing and pointing at her. She turned her face back to the wind and let it dry the tears that streaked down her dusty face. Oh, she would get her revenge. Jake thought he was so funny. Well, she would see just how funny he was when the joke was on him!

That night after supper, her father retired to the porch with a snifter of whiskey. She straightened up the kitchen and slowly crept out the back door. She walked over to the barn and found her horse's stall. Shadow was a good five and a half hands tall. He was a chestnut with a black mane and tail. She took a piece of rope and quickly made a bridle for him. She levered herself onto his back and walked him out of the barn toward the pond and Jake. She knew that Jake went swimming in the pond on hot summer nights. And Ray would bet a whole pot of silver dollars that he was there tonight.

As Shadow neared the pond, she stopped by a thicket of trees to see if she was right. Yep, he was there, and he was alone. She knew the tree that he tied his horse to and hung his clothes on while he swam. As she made her way over to his horse, she finalized her plan. He was out in chest deep water. He was breathing pretty hard, so he must have been making laps from one side to the other. When he saw her, he started making his way up to shore, but being a respectful boy, he wouldn't come out with her looking at him. That was a big mistake! She called to him, "Jake, do you know what makes revenge so sweet?"

Jake took on the look of someone knowing he was going to have to pay for something he didn't deserve.

"Now, Ray, you know that was an accident. If you would have waited and not run off like a baby, I would have bought you some more candy," he said.

Immediately realizing the term *baby* was not a good one, Ray responded, "Well, I don't believe that! You would have took the opportunity to make more fun of me as usual. And now it looks like I'm just going to have to make a joke out of you. Try not to cry like a baby."

She edged closer to his clothes hanging on the tree, and his eyes widened. "You can't mean to take my clothes. Now that is a very dirty, low down thing to do, Ray."

As she reached the tree, she lifted his clothes onto the back of her horse. Jake came out of the water a little further. The water was just below his belly button. He stopped and tried one last time. "Ray, now you don't want to do that. You know it was an accident."

Ray let a low smile cross her face and said, "Don't worry, Jake. I'm sure you'll be fine. After all, it was only an accident. Just give it time, and I'm sure everything will be right as rain!" As she turned her horse to leave, he rushed out of the water. Too late, a quick kick to Shadows flank had her kicking up dust in his face.

Darn that girl. Now how am I going to get home? He had no choice but to suck it up and ride his horse back to the ranch. Too bad the wind wasn't warmer. It wouldn't have been so bad. By the time he made it back to the ranch, he was shaking, and his lips were turning blue. That girl was meaner than a rattle snake and twice as deadly. He would never forgive her for making a fool of him. He decided he would steer clear of her from now on.

That night when Ray went up to her room, she tossed off her dirty pants and shirt and slipped on her white cotton night gown and climbed into bed. She felt really pleased with herself. *I'm sure Jake didn't think that was very funny*, she laughed to herself. Having to ride back to the ranch butt naked would sure hurt his pride and make him think twice about messing with her! The last thing she saw before she fell asleep was the look on Jake's face when she took off with his clothes! She slept soundly with a great big ole' smile on her face.

CHAPTER 1

Odessa, Texas
1921

"Good job, Ray. Keep your head down. Hold on!" Sam called to her from the corral fence. Rayne had been trying to break the large black stud horse for the last four hours. Finally he was starting to tire out. The horse swung around and lurched forward one last time. He stopped bucking, and with heavy breaths, he started walking slowly around the corral with his head down. Ray heaved a sigh of relief, thanking God. She didn't know how much more she could have handled. The black brute had thrown her two times, and she had the bruises to prove it. However, now he had given in and would become another smooth-riding animal. "All right, Ray!" the other hands shouted to her and cheered from the fence.

Her father waved to her with a smile on his face. She had once again tamed the mustang. He was happy for her. He could not look at his daughter and not feel joy for her many accomplishments, and God knew there were several; but as he covered his mouth for the cough that heaved in his chest, he knew he was getting weaker by the day. A new face was in town by the name of Clay Elliot. And he was quickly buying up all the land around these parts. He had made Bob several offers on his place, but he knew without a doubt Ray would not accept him selling out. She loved the ranch with all of her heart and would accept nothing less than owning it herself one day. He had tried to reason with her that the ranch was a lot of work, and she would need someone to share the burden with at the end of the day. She had reacted as he expected and through clenched teeth told him she didn't need a husband. She had Sam, and they could run the ranch together. It never occurred to her that Sam was as old as him and would not be there forever either. Bob gave up trying to talk to her about the subject. Ray had grown into a beautiful woman. She was nineteen now. She had grown to a healthy five feet seven inches tall. She had a lean build, long legs, and slightly wide hips that were not flattered by her father's old pants and button-up shirts. Her hair was a light red and a mass of curls. She kept it wound up into a bun under her cowboy hat. She wouldn't even consider a dress these days.

Ray climbed off the exhausted horse equally tired herself. She had done it. And she would not let her aching muscles damper her happiness. She could do anything on the ranch as good as or better than any of the other guys. And her father would not accept it. She loved her father, but his constant reminder that she was of age and needed a husband continued to grate on her nerves. She knew he had an old-fashioned view of a woman's place on a ranch, but surely, he could see that did not apply to her. She assumed if she had had her mother to influence her, she would have become a different woman, but she hadn't. Those dreams of frilly dresses and tea parties were long gone for her. She had to grow up and needed to be strong for her father. He loved this ranch and had worked very hard over the years to keep it in the black and prospering.

She walked out of the corral and crossed to the house. Stepping into the kitchen in the back, she fixed herself a glass of sweet tea and sat at the table. She could hear her father out on the porch. His cough was getting worse. The strain of the dry heat and dust was causing him to get weaker every day. She would not face the truth she knew was coming. She refused to believe her father's days were numbered and avoided his talk of getting old. She had lost her mother but was determined not to lose her father. God wouldn't be that cruel, would he? What child wouldn't want to believe her father was going to live forever? Of course she was not a child anymore and had not been for a long time, but she still held on to the dream that her father was invincible. She believed her father would sign over the ranch to her before he would sell out, but Clay had been making several visits as well as offers. He had even tried to court her, finding out very quick she was not interested. He abandoned the idea of making a match with her to take over the ranch. He was not a bad-looking man. He was tall with blonde hair, blue eyes, and a lanky build. But Ray could not get past the idea that he loved his whiskey as much as buying up land.

She remembered the night he had come calling; her father had convinced her to take a ride with him. She hadn't done anything different to her appearance, and he didn't seem to mind. When they had gotten out of sight of the ranch, he told her he had big plans for them. He would marry her and take over the running of the ranch. She would have to learn to cook, but he didn't care if she took the less glamorous chores like mucking the stalls and straightening up the house. He also decided she would provide him with an heir and tried to get a start on that. She had slapped his face when he tried to kiss her. After the first shock of the slap, he had raised his hand to strike her back, but she was too fast. She had blocked the blow and had no trouble connecting her fist with his nose. He had driven her back to the ranch in silence. Her father was sitting in the swing on the porch when they got back. With a great deal of effort, he had managed not to laugh. When Clay rode off, she didn't tell her father what had happened even though she knew he had a good idea. She simply said, "Don't think he'll be calling again." Her father had nodded and went back to swinging. She was right of course. He had not come to court her again, but he would not give up on the idea of buying the ranch. Her father had over a thousand acres which bordered one of the ranches Clay had already purchased. Her father's ranch also bordered the Rocking J on the west line. There was a large pond right in the middle of the line separating the two ranches. Because it was on the line and neither one would give the other total rights to it, they shared the water between the two.

She loved that pond and enjoyed wading out into it on those moonlight summer nights. She would let the water wash the layers of tension from her tired muscles one at a time. She also had fond memories of that pond and of stealing Jake Hale's clothes one night after he had made fun of her. She wondered what Jake looked like now. It had been eight years since she had seen him. Just weeks after the incident at the pond, Jake had gone off to his uncle's house in

Philadelphia. She figured he would one day come back to the ranch, but she couldn't help but wonder if he liked city life better. She had never admitted that she had a crush on Jake. She would take that little secret to her grave, but it didn't stop her mind from wondering if he was married yet and what his bride looked like. Obviously, not anything like her! She would be shorter with blonde hair hanging in ringlets around her face. She would wear big frilly dresses and fan herself with an over joyous smile.

She couldn't deny she had no intentions of ever wearing dresses and big fancy hats, especially not sitting there sipping tea and sharing the gossip with a bunch of other ladies. She had heard that Jim, Jake's father, had taken a fall off a horse and injured his back. She didn't know how bad the injury was but wondered if it was bad enough to call his only son back from the big city. The Rocking J ranch was a little larger than her father's, but they ran about the same number of cattle. They also had good contracts selling horses. They would round up a bunch of mustangs, brand them, and then start the tiresome task of breaking them one by one. She knew all too well what it was like to try and break a mustang's spirit. She had just defeated one earlier today, and it was no easy task. It had taken her a week to calm him before she was even able to touch him. She knew how he felt and understood his fear better than anyone. Her father had been trying long enough to get her to give some of the brave callers a chance to break her spirit, but in the end, she triumphed. She wondered how much longer she could hold out. Even though she was very happy working with her father and Sam, sometimes, she longed for someone to talk to on another level. Someone she could share her emotions with and lean on when she lost all energy to get up and do it another day. Maybe someday she would find someone who could stand her boyish ways enough to see the woman inside of her instead of only seeing the tomboy on the outside. She prayed she would be able to handle a relationship if God decided to send one her way. He knew she was head strong and not easy to deal with; so maybe he would send her someone who liked a fight!

CHAPTER 2

Philadelphia, Pennsylvania
1921

Jake stood to the side of the dance floor watching as the laughing couples swirled together. Charlie, his friend from school, stood beside him. "Why don't you go ask Rebecca to dance? She has been staring at you all evening. Did you two have a fight?" Charlie said between drinks of his sherry.

Jake turned toward Charlie with a blank face. "I don't want to dance. All I can think about is that she is expecting me to propose." He took a deep breath and went on. "I don't love her. We have had a good time these past few months, but it is hard to picture her back on the ranch. She would definitely wilt in the heat of Texas."

Charlie pondered his statement and said, "Why do you have to go back to the ranch? You could stay here and settle down." Looking like he had solved all Jake's problems, he smiled smugly and said, "Are you really worried about the ranch or the word marriage?"

Jake thought about it a moment and replied, "I know I will get married someday, but I want to return to Texas and take over the ranch for my father. I guess I always planned to find a wife that was accustomed to the heat and hard work." Jake looked around the room at all the porcelain faces. Rebecca was a sweet girl, but she was getting very demanding. They had been courting for a few months now, and she was dead set on his proposal. He was sure she would not be so excited to be his bride if she knew he would be running a cattle ranch in Texas. He had no doubt after one day she would run screaming to the nearest train station. Texas was not a place for the fragile Rebecca. He needed a strong woman who would work beside him and enjoy what they had made together. Yes, he thought strong and soft; she would need to be able to stay calm and handle whatever came at her, a necessity when running a ranch. She would need enough energy to keep up with him in the daytime and enough passion to keep him sated at night. He knew he would have more luck asking the wind to change directions than finding a woman that had all those qualities.

"Mr. Hale?" the young man asked again.

Jake looked at him with distracted eyes. "Yes. Can I be of some assistance to you?" Jake asked.

"I have a message for you. I believe it concerns your father. It was brought here by a messenger from your aunt. She says it is very urgent."

Jake took the piece of paper from his hands and absently thanked him. As she opened, it he saw it was a telegraph from Odessa. It had been sent from his mother and simply read: "Come. There has been an accident." It took him all of two seconds to read the telegraph and took about the same amount of time to get his evening coat and hat from the doorman. When he reached his aunt's house, he packed a small case and told her he was leaving immediately. She had not expected any less he supposed after reading the message his mother had sent. He instructed his aunt to send a telegraph to his mother in the morning explaining that he had received the message and was already on the train back to Texas. He hailed a buggy to the train station and within hours was tucked into a seat on the train for the long ride home.

When the train let out a loud series of whistles, Jake woke with a start. He set up in the seat, tried to straighten the creases out of his coat and vest, and ran his hands through his hair. The train ride had not been an easy one, especially when all his thoughts were focused on the accident his mother had written of. When the whistle blew another set of short warnings, he knew they were approaching the platform. He stood up and reached for his case.

As the train rolled to a stop in front of the station, he walked up the hallway to the steps. As he descended to the platform, he took a deep breath of that fresh hot air. He had missed this ole dust bowl.

He laughed to himself and walked to the side of the ticket building. He expected his mother would send one of the ranch hands to pick him up, but as he came around the corner, he saw no one he recognized. A few yards away from the station were the rows of buildings that made up the town of Odessa, Texas, he had grown up running these streets with a gang of his friends. They would beg their fathers for money to buy candy and drinks at Baker's General Store then hide out behind the barber shop and shoot stones from their sling shots at the empty bottles. They never grew tired of sneaking around the saloon and laughing at the drunken men stumbling around and, of course, the pretty women in low-cut dresses.

He walked over to Baker General Store and was a little surprised to find Mr. Baker still running it; he was standing in the doorway giving orders to a young man stacking flour bags when Jake walked up. "Hello, Mr. Baker. You sure haven't changed much, still stacking your flour bags the same way I see," Jake said to him with a wide smile on his face. "Well, hey there, Jake. I didn't expect to see you back here. This young man here who is eager to learn is Josh Barnwell. He is working for me for a few weeks. My Elsa has taken sick and can't help me in the store anymore."

"I'm sorry, Mr. Baker. I hope Mrs. Elsa gets to feeling better soon," Jake said with a somber smile. He knew Mrs. Elsa had been sick for a while now. His mother had written to him that she had taken ill and was getting weaker by the day. He could see the sadness in the older man's eyes. It really was hard to go on day by day and watch the woman you have loved for years just waste away. As he was about to help the poor boy out, he heard a wagon drawing up in front of the store. He turned to look at the driver, and as the wagon stopped, he thought the man looked familiar. He wore an older cowboy hat stained around the front with sweat. His shirt was a simple button-down cotton shirt with the sleeves rolled up to his elbow. His pants were just as simple, cut large as not to cling to his lean frame; they were two sizes too big and cinched at the waist with a belt. As the man stepped out of the wagon, he turned toward Jake. In that instant, shock consumed him. His mouth fell open, and he could not believe his eyes. The man was not a man. The man was a woman with freckles along the bridge of her nose, and as she walked closer, he could see the slight outline of curves in all the right places. Her clothes were almost large enough to hide her very feminine figure. But her tan-freckled face was clearly visible beneath the brim of the hat.

"Shut your mouth, Jake. You're going to catch flies." The feisty statement definitely proved who she was, but he could not bring himself to believe the lanky, rotten little girl had grown into such a beautiful woman even though she was wearing her father's hand-me-downs. He was going to say something, anything at all; but when he tried to talk, he found his throat closed up. He cleared his throat loudly and gave it another shot. "Ray, you sure have changed. I didn't recognize you in that outfit," Jake said.

She dragged her eyes over the length of him and said, "You look different to. Like a city boy." She smiled widely and walked on into the store.

"Mr. Baker, did you get the items I requested?" Ray asked, looking around the store. She saw Josh hastily trying to keep his eyes on the flour sacks and not her. She knew the little runt had a crush on her. She had been nice to him, always gave him a few cents tip for loading up the wagon for her. She smiled at him and gave him a wink. Oh, what good was living if you couldn't have a little fun? Jake stood outside the doorway to the store. He was still trying to wrap his mind around the idea that Ray was all grown up. Had he really been away that long? As he was trying to picture her in his mind again, another buggy drove up.

It was J. W. the foreman at his father's ranch. He walked down the steps and crossed to the buggy. "Sorry, I wasn't here when your train came in. We were a little unsure which one you were on." J. W. tipped his hat to Jake as he slung his case in the back and climbed in.

"That's okay. It gave me some time to visit with Mr. Baker and to get the shock of my life at seeing Ray." Jake looked toward the doorway of the store and nodded to Mr. Baker as they started off. The town was the same all right, but some people had definitely changed. As the buggy headed out of town, he chanced a look back toward the store and saw Ray, Mr. Baker, and little Josh standing on the porch laughing.

CHAPTER 3

Jake sat looking out in the distance at the mountains rising up out of the parched ground. God sure outdone himself when he made Texas. It was the middle of June and was starting to feel like full-blown August. The wind was strong and blew straight into his face. He had never felt happier to be home. He was dreading arriving at the ranch and finding his family in turmoil. He knew his mother would be uneasy about his coming home. He thought she would have known that he preferred the ranch to the city. He had always been happiest at the ranch. He sent her letters from Philadelphia often, and he always tried to make it sound like he was having a good time. He even wrote to her of Rebecca and the friendship they had made, leaving out that she had already planned to be his bride. He couldn't imagine himself marrying someone other than a rancher's daughter; they would be tougher and understand how things worked. He was going to find him someone who could share the ups and downs and be happy about it.

As the wagon pulled up to the house, his mother stepped out of the door onto the porch. She was four feet eight inches of pure beauty. Her blonde hair had started to bud with grey. Not something, he noted, that made her look old. But instead, she looked proud standing there with a white handkerchief pressed into her hand and fighting back tears for her only son. He climbed out of the wagon and rushed to her. He embraced her in a strong bear hug. He pulled back and smiled into her face. The first tear slipped down her cheek, and he took the handkerchief from her and wiped it away. "I'm here now, Mama." He spoke softly, watching her soft lips form a smile.

"I'm so sorry to have called you back, Jackson. But it simply couldn't be helped," she said, her voice a little shaky. He embraced her again. He rubbed his hands up and down her arms.

"What has happened?" he asked her. She pulled away from him and started in the house.

"Come on," she called back to him as she headed down the hallway and into the study. He slipped into the house and closed the door behind him. He walked slowly toward the study door. When he turned the corner, he stood, eyes wide and motionless as his gaze fell on his father sitting next to a side table in what looked like a wheelchair.

His father's eyes never left his face. He watched in silent horror as Jake took in his appearance and guessed at what had left him without the use of his legs. Jim Hale was a tall man, lean and muscular from years of hard work. The sun had turned his skin a light brown and had hardened the lines of his face to the look of leather. He did not smile or show any emotion on his face, but you could see his sharp blue eyes calculating the reaction to the fragile look of the rough and tough cowboy he had always been.

"Father, how—" Jake felt his control start to break. "How?" was all Jake could force out of his mouth from his suddenly dry throat. Jake moved to his father and took a knee in front of him. He took his hand in his and waited for him to explain what had happened. Jake could see the embarrassment in his father's nervous face. He knew it was hard for him to sit there and not be able to pace as he always had when he told the details of a story. Jim cleared his throat and looked at Jake.

"Son, these things happen, I'm told. But it is never easy when you're the one it happens too. I was riding Jasper along the fence line. I caught sight of some strays. As I set Jasper to a run, I didn't see the washout. Jasper went down and buckled backward on top of me.

"I laid there for several hours. The old horse thrashed around in panic until J. W. and the boys came to check on me. When they found me, they hauled Jasper out of the hole. He had broken two of his legs trying to paw his way out, and they had to put him down.

"They got me out of the hole, and I couldn't stand. I still can't feel or move my legs. I can't even wiggle my damn toes! The doctor said I injured some of the nerves in my back and may never be able to use my legs again."

Jake stared at his father. He knew Jasper was his favorite horse and one of the first he had broken after he took over the ranch from his father. "I'm sorry about Jasper, father. I know he meant a lot to you." Jake waited for a response but only saw despair.

"Jake, I'm sorry to have to take you away from your schooling, but we need you here. You have to take over the ranch, son. It's your place. I hope you can understand that."

Jake smiled at his father, hoping to ease the anxiety of condemning his only son to a life of ranching. "Father, I have always dreamed of taking over the ranch one day. There are no hard feelings for having to come home from school. I would rather be here any day as to be in the city. Surely, you know that." Jake looked at his father and saw a hint of a smile.

Jim looked to his wife and said, "See, Sarah? I told you he would take it like a champ."

Sarah spoke softly. "Jake, are you sure you don't mind coming back home for good? What about your friends and that nice girl Rebecca you spoke of?" Jake looked up at his mother.

"No, Mom, it will not be a problem to take over the ranch, and I'm sure Rebecca can find other gentleman to entertain her."

Sarah smiled. "Well, if you are certain."

"I am," Jake replied. Jake rose and kissed his mother's cheek. "Have you spoken to J. W. about this, father?" Jim looked at Jake.

"It is your place to speak with them now, boss." Jim added with a smile.

Jake excused himself and walked toward the doorway. "I guess I should get started," he said.

Jake walked out of the front door and started toward the barn. J. W. and the boys were sitting at the table in the bunkhouse next to the barn. They had settled down for a game of poker. Jake walked in, and all heads turned. "Boys, it looks like I am your new boss. If you have any questions, problems, or concerns about the Rocking J, they should be directed to me," Jake said with the tip of his hat. The boys looked around the table at each other and then back to Jake.

J. W. stood and stretched out his hand for congratulations. "It will be a pleasure to work for you, Jake. Just like it has been to work for your father."

One of the hands put in. "Yeah, we are all just sick about what happened to your father."

Jake smiled and looked to all the ranch hands. "Thanks, guys, I appreciate that. I'm sure we will get along just fine."

All the boys tipped their hats and toasted Jake with a shot of whiskey. Jake took one himself and tried not to cough as the liquid slid down his dry throat, leaving a trail of fire behind. Jake declined offers to join in the game and turned to J. W.

"I'm going to go for a ride. Which horse should I take?"

J. W. considered a moment. There were several good horses to choose from and with a smile replied, "Take that Sorrell in the first stall. That was the last horse your father broke before he got hurt."

Jake turned for the door and replied, "I appreciate that, J. W." and walked out the door and headed to the barn.

He walked inside and looked toward the first stall and saw the gorgeous animal staring back at him. Jake walked over and opened the stall door. Walking in, he took the mare by her rope halter and walked her out to the hallway of the barn. She didn't give him any trouble while he saddled her up or mounted. She took his commands well and walked out of the barn. Jake roamed the fence line and took in the scenery he had missed for the last several years. He spent some time thanking God for sparing his father's life. His father may not agree right now, but it was God's mercy that saved him. As the sun started getting low, the sweat that had been soaking his shirt all day reminded him of the pond, and he could think of nothing better than a cool late night dip. As he neared the pines that skirted the pond, he could hear splashing and had no idea of the surprise he was about to get.

He slowed his horse, climbed out of the saddle, and tied her to a nearby tree. He walked quietly up to the trees and peered out at the water. He could not believe his eyes. There was a gorgeous woman swimming in his pond. She had dark waves of long hair and a gorgeous tanned face. By the way the moonlight glowed on her skin, he would swear she was a dream. She turned toward him and dived down deep in the water. He could see the swell of her backside as she plunged down. When she pushed back out of the water, she was facing him and had a big smile on her face. He sunk lower behind the tree, hoping she hadn't spotted him. She started swimming toward the bank, and he noticed her clothes hanging on the low tree branch. As she got to the shallow water, she stood up. She was completely naked! Jake turned his back to the tree. *Dear God, this woman is bold*, he thought. Praying she hadn't heard him, he silently waited for her to get dressed; she walked out of the water and reached for her clothes. She pulled her shirt and pants on. He risked a glance and saw that she was finally clothed. She threw her hair to the side and started to wring it out. Her small hands worked efficiently to squeeze the water out, and it puddled at her bare feet. She sat down on the bank and pulled on her boots. Without a backward glance, she whistled for her horse. When he trotted over, she hopped in the saddle and tore out.

Jake stared at her disappearing figure and the cloud of long hair that followed. Then it struck him: the only other person of his age that had use of the pond was Rayne Whitmore. Holy cow, that girl had matured into a beautiful woman! He broke through the trees and walked over to the pond. He stripped off his clothes and boots and waded in. The cool water was a welcomed relief to his body. God knows he needed this to take the fire out of his blood for the girl he had just spied on. How could he have these feelings for Ray? She had humiliated him every chance she got and didn't care to do it again after all these years. He lay back in the water and began to backstroke, hoping the weightlessness of the water would help to clear his head. God forgive him, but it took everything he had not to wade out into that water with her. She probably would have clawed his eyes out, but it would have been worth it. Seems running this ranch was going to have some benefits after all!

CHAPTER 4

Rayne stood in the kitchen, mixing a bowl of biscuits. She had decided when she got up this morning that she was going to surprise Emma with a request for cooking lessons. Emma was Sam's devoted wife of thirty-two years. She was in her fifties with a plump face and plump build to match. She had grey hair she gathered up in a bun on top of her head and was the sweetest person Ray had ever known. She had indeed surprised Emma as she had stood there with a grin on her face; Ray even had to convince her she was not joking. She tied on an apron and started getting down a bowl and spoon. Now she was mixing the flour and eggs to Emma's directions. Ray didn't fully understand why she took a notion to learn how to cook, but she was sure with Emma teaching her, she would enjoy it. Emma had made every effort to nurture Ray after her mother had died, and now Ray wished she had let her have her way in some things. If she hadn't been so pig headed and stubborn, she might have learned to cook several years ago.

Bob came down the stairs at the smell of brewing coffee and bacon frying. He could hear two women chatting and figured Ray was up and already started on breakfast. He walked into the kitchen and couldn't believe his eyes. Ray stood stock still, meeting her father's bewildered gaze and smiled. Bob was shocked. Ray had never been interested in cooking, and now here she stood, mixing a bowl of flour and eggs. Her hair was hanging down in auburn curls around her shoulders. She had flour dotted on her nose and cheeks and a large grin on her face.

Bob walked across the floor and stood in front of Ray. Turning his head to Emma, he said, "Emma, what do you think? Has our girl came down with the fever?" Emma just grinned and said nothing.

He turned back to Ray and said very slow for extra emphasis, "Ray, are you sure you're feeling okay this morning? Do you know where you are?"

Ray looked at her father and grinned wide. Without a word, she dipped her hand into the flour bowl and grabbed a hand full of flour. She brought her hand back out and threw the flour at him, covering his face. Bob let out a long breath, absently blowing flour in the air. Without a word, he dipped his hand in the flour bowl and threw some flour back into Ray's face.

Ray stood shocked silently watching her father. Emma broke out laughing. Ray and her father both dipped their hands in the bowl together and threw flour in Emma's laughing face. She stopped laughing and scowled at both of them. Emma had a basket of eggs sitting on the counter. She reached in and got two eggs out. Holding one over each head, she smashed them down on top of Ray and her father. Emma started howling with laughter again. Ray and her father could not stand it any longer. They also started laughing. Sam came through the back door with someone behind him. "Good God! What happened in here?" Sam asked with a look at all three flour-and-egg-covered faces.

Emma cleared her throat and turned to Sam. "I am giving Ray a cooking lesson."

Sam looked at Ray and started laughing. "Well, I guess it could have been worse. Honey, I know this is your first lesson, but the flour and eggs go in the bowl! Don't worry, you'll get it right eventually!" Sam started laughing again. Ray once again dipped her hand into the bowl. Emma saw the look on her face and knew what was fixing to happen. She side stepped Sam and moved out of the way. With a little shriek, Ray heaved the hand full of flour at Sam.

Unfortunately, Sam was paying attention and moved out of the way just in time for the flour to smack the figure behind him in the face. Ray gasped and rushed forward, muttering apologies. She took the rag Emma offered and started to wipe the man's face off. He stood very still and didn't make a sound as Ray tried desperately to wipe his face clean. When she made the swipe across his eyes and nose, she saw bright green eyes staring back at her. As the rag came across his firm lips, she saw him grin. In that instant, she knew who the man was.

Ray spoke slowly and kept her eyes on Jake's face. "Well, it looks like you have a habit of being in the wrong place at the wrong time." Ray had kept the joy of hitting him with the flour contained long enough. She threw back her head and laughed right in his face. Jake looked to the flour-covered faces, and Sam then turned back to Ray. Before she knew what was happening, Jake picked her up and headed out the back door with her in his arms. Ray started kicking her feet and slapping wildly. She was screaming for Jake to put her down.

When he stopped suddenly, a wide grin spread across his face. He stared into her eyes for a couple seconds just long enough for Ray to see the mischief in them. Jake abruptly removed his arms from under her, and Ray was falling. With a loud splash, Ray landed in the water tank beside the corral fence. Ray gasped with shock. The water was freezing.

When she came back to the top of the water, she could see Jake standing beside the tank laughing! His face still had flour around the edges, and it was in his hair. What kind of person would she be if she didn't help him clean it up? She feigned pain and flopped in the water a little. Jake immediately noticed and leaned over the water tank to help her out. She grabbed the front of his shirt and pulled with all her weight. Jake landed in the tank on top of her. She hadn't planned on his weight pushing her under again. She wrapped her arms around his waist and tried to turn him, so she could get some air. When he realized what she was doing, he put his hands on her shoulders and pulled her toward him bringing her face out of the water. Ray gasped for air and filled her lungs; she turned her face toward Jake. She was almost nose to nose with him. She could see his green eyes smoldering. She didn't know if it was because of anger or something else. When he licked his lips slowly, she knew.

"I should have let you drown, you hellcat!" Jake said through his teeth. Before she could react to his name calling, he moved his hands from her shoulders to around her waist. She looked into his eyes again and knew exactly what she saw there, desire! She started to struggle, but it was too late. Jake pulled her hard up against him and pressed his lips to hers, angry at first and then softening in to silk. So sweet and soft. She was determined not to return his kiss even though her whole body was starting to warm from deep within her, a small fire growing outward and consuming her whole body. Jake slowly opened his mouth and ran his tongue across her bottom lip. She gasped, giving him the opening he wanted. Once his tongue was in her mouth, she had no more thoughts. The only thing that mattered was this wild man with his arms around her and his tongue exploring her mouth. She suddenly threw herself into the kiss. Moving her hands up to around his neck and plunging her fingers into his hair, Jake knew the instant she started responding to his kiss. He moved his head to the side deepening the kiss, and she clung to him and molded herself to him as much as was possible in the water. He drew the kiss out as long as he could, but the water was freezing. He pulled back slowly and heard her sigh of protest. He looked into her flushed face and saw her eyes closed. She slowly opened her eyes and looked up at him. The crimson on her cheeks turned a deeper red.

Slowly, the world started to come back. Ray turned toward the house and saw her father, Sam, and Emma all standing a few steps out of the house but close enough to get an eye full of what just happened. It seemed Emma was frozen in shock. Her handkerchief pressed to her mouth. Her father was standing still with his arms crossed over his chest. Sam was standing next to him with a similar pose. She swore under her breath and shoved Jake back off her enough she could stand up. She jumped out of the water trough and run into the house.

Jake was still a little shocked. He struggled to get himself out of the water. He stepped out and turned to the smiling faces watching. "I'm sorry, Bob. I didn't plan on that happening," Jake said, trying to shake some of the water from his drenched clothes.

"That's okay, Jake. Sometimes, you just have to go with your gut," Bob said, still smiling.

"I don't think Ray will have that same opinion." Jake spat out trying to keep from shaking.

"Come on in. We will get you some dry clothes, and you can join us for breakfast." Bob turned and started into the house. Bob led Jake upstairs and got him some dry clothes. "You can change in here," he told Jake as he started out the bedroom door, closing it behind him. Jake pulled his wet clothes off and let them pool on the wood floor. He couldn't help but think of Ray doing the same. He knew there was only one wall separating them and for an instant thought of charging into her room and insisting they finished what they started; God help him. The woman tempted him.

Ray would be madder than a wet hen. He had unintentionally embarrassed her in front of everyone she cared about. He had never felt a shock like that from just one kiss, and surely, she could feel his body reacting to hers as she had pressed herself so tight up against him. He knew Ray would never admit she had a part in what had happened out there. He finished dressing and walked back down stairs. Ray was not down stairs when he got there. She was undoubtedly still sulking in her room. Jake refused the offers for breakfast and made his escape. He had come to a decision. Ray would not have anything to do with him right now, but she couldn't resist him forever. With time and a lot of luck, he would find a way to see her, and they would figure out what this attraction was between them whether she liked it or not!

CHAPTER 5

Ray had been working hard all day; she had rounded up cattle for branding, run a heard of wild horses into the corral for working, and she was seriously give out. She unsaddled her horse and brushed him down. When she finished, she turned and started to the house. Where was her father? He had excused himself from working with her today, saying he had some business to take care of in town. She wondered just what sort of business he was tending to in the middle of the workday.

Bob steered the wagon through the gate of the Rocking J ranch. He pulled up to the house and climbed down. When he reached the door, Sarah was standing in the door way. "Hello, Bob. How are you today?" Sarah said with a smile as she stepped back from the doorway for Bob to enter.

"Just fine, Sarah. Thank you for asking. I was hoping to have a word with Jim if he's not busy." Bob said, smiling to Sarah. He watched several emotions play across her face before she controlled them and smiled again.

"Sure, he is in the study. Right this way." Sarah led the way to the study and, while he waited outside the door, told Jim that Bob was there to see him. She came back into the hallway and motioned for Bob to enter. He was stunned for a moment as he took in Jim's appearance and the wheelchair he was sitting in. He was gazing out the window and didn't acknowledge that Bob had come into the room.

Bob cleared his throat, "Hello, Jim, I was hoping you would have a couple minutes to speak with me."

Jim shrugged his shoulders and answered, "I don't have any-thing else to do, so why not?"

Bob crossed the room and took the chair beside Jim. He cleared his throat again before he went on. "Jim, I know Jake came home to run the ranch for you. And I'm proud you have a son that can inherit yours, but the point is, we are both getting older and our health is fading. I don't know how much longer I am going to be around. Clay has been hounding me again pretty hard, and I'm sure he's paid you a visit too."

Jim just nodded his head. Bob went on. "I worry about Ray after I'm gone and what I should do with the ranch since I don't have a son to take over and Ray is not married." He paused a minute before he went on. Jim was giving him his attention, and he wondered how he would take this next part. "Jim, you know if Clay gets control of my ranch, he will make it hell on you until he can force Jake to sell out. The pond is peacefully shared because our fathers reached an agreement, and we have been able to honor it. But it will not be that easy to deal with if an outsider takes over."

Jim looked at Bob. "Get to the point. I'm sure you didn't come over here to tell me what I already know."

Bob shook his head. "You're right. I am stalling. I've got a proposition for you. Before you say no, just hear me out." Jim nodded, and he went on, "You have a son, and I have a daughter. If we could combine the two ranches in say, a wedding, there would not be any reason to worry about our ranches falling into someone else's hands." Bob paused and looked at Jim. Jim had a thoughtful look on his face.

He turned to Bob and said, "You probably don't know this, but I had an arranged marriage to my Sarah. I have never regretted my decision, but Jake and Ray are in a different situation. Do you honestly think Ray would agree to a marriage, especially to my Jake? Those two have been at each other's throats since they were old enough to ride."

Bob didn't have to think about it. "Well, what I saw this morning made me think this could be possible. They accidentally wound up necking in our watering trough. I'm certain Ray will come around when her only two choices are to sell out to Clay or marry Jake. So she can keep the ranch, she will do whatever she has to too keep the ranch. I'm positive!" Bob looked at Jim and asked, "What about Jake? How will he feel about this?"

"He will do what is necessary, I'm sure. He loves this ranch as much as Ray loves yours."

Bob smiled, "Well, okay then. I will speak to Ray about this when I get back home." Jim nodded, "Sarah and I will speak to Jake about this. Why don't you and Ray come up here for supper tonight?" Jim smiled. "It will be interesting to see how the two of them react to being engaged to each other."

"I agree," Bob said. He excused himself from the room and headed back to his wagon. He smiled and tipped his hat to Sarah as he passed the kitchen. The road back to his ranch had gotten shorter, and he was a little worried about how Ray was going to take the news that he had offered her to Jake to save the ranch. One thing he was sure of, there would be fireworks at the ranch tonight!

When Bob arrived home, Ray was sitting in the kitchen talking to Emma. Bob walked in and took a seat at the table across from Ray. He cleared his throat, drawing the attention to him. Both women turned and looked at him. "I have an announcement to make." Bob started and was pleased to see he had the full attention of both women. "There is going to be a wedding very soon." He saw both faces fill with curiosity and went on. "Jake is getting married." The single statement brought a surprised shock from both of them. *This was it*, he thought, *preparing to run if need be.* He slowly stated, "He is marrying you, Ray!" The curiosity drained from her face replaced first by shock and then laughter.

It took Ray a few seconds before she could speak. She was laughing so hard. "Dad, a little kiss this morning does not mean we have to get married. Do not get in such a hurry to marry me off!"

Bob smiled. "I am not *trying* to marry you off. I arranged it! Jim and I came to a decision that will solve both our problems and take a lot of worry off of us. You and Jake get married, combining the two ranches, and Clay will never be able to get the both of you to sell. But if you two stay separate, either Jake or you could be convinced to sell if things get much worse. This way, the two people who can take care of these ranches the best will be running them *together*."

Ray considered this for a few minutes and softly replied, "So you're saying either I marry Jake, or I don't get the ranch. Is that right?" Ray looked at her father waiting for his answer.

"Yes, that's right." Ray looked stunned for a minute. Then she composed her features. "Jake will never agree to it. He can't stand the sight of me. He will never agree to marry me."

Bob looked very smug as he said, "Don't worry, honey. He already has. Now go upstairs and put something ladylike on. We are going up there for supper tonight." Ray closed her eyes and took a deep breath, trying to calm the storm brewing within her from this news.

"Okay, father, whatever you say." Surely, she could talk some sense into Jake. They wouldn't have to marry to keep their ranches. That was crazy! Just like two old men to start thinking up crazy ideas like that. She excused herself from the table and started up the stairs. She stopped and turned back toward her father. "I will need a dress to wear. I don't have any."

Her father spoke softly. "Your mother's dresses are in the trunk in my room. Help yourself."

With a huff, she turned and headed up the stairs. Emma came upstairs shortly after and offered to help Ray dress. She knew it had been a very long time since Ray had worn a dress and was sure she would need some help. She found Ray in her room looking at three dresses she had gotten out of the trunk. She knocked softly on the door and walked in. Ray was sitting on the bed and looked up at her. "I thought you might need some help getting ready." Emma smiled at Ray, and as she stood up, she lifted one of the dresses off the bed.

"I think I will wear this one." She ran her hand down the front of the dress. "It always was my favorite on Mama." Emma stepped over to Ray and took the dress from her hands.

"It is beautiful, honey. Are you sure you're okay with this? It is a lot to process in a very short time. You seem to be handling it exceptionally well."

Ray turned to face Emma. "Emma, I have decided I don't have anything to worry about. There is no way Jake would agree to marry me. He can't stand me." She said, lifting her chin. Emma cleared her throat. "I got the impression this morning when the two of you tangled up in the water tank that he seems to like you at least a little bit!"

Ray blushed and rolled her eyes. "That doesn't matter. He told dad he didn't mean it."

Emma smiled. Ray really had no idea what she was getting into. If it had not mattered, he would have not kissed her so passionately. She had no idea what was going to be in store for her when she got to Jake's house tonight. Emma rushed to get her dressed and pulled her tangle of curls up on top of her head, letting a few curls escape and slip down her neck and the sides of her face. With one last look at Ray and the beauty she had become, she slipped out and went back downstairs. Ray would need time to think out her plan. Emma just hoped Jake was wise enough to guess what he was going to be faced with when Ray and her father arrived.

CHAPTER 6

Ray and her father arrived at Jake's house just before sundown. They were greeted by Sarah at the front door. They followed her into the study where Jim and Jake were waiting. When Ray walked into the room, a slow smile spread across Jim's face. Ray blushed and smoothed the skirts of her dress. She looked back at Jim, taking in the quilt over his lap and the wheelchair he was sitting in. She tried to hide the shock from her face. Jake cleared his throat and stepped toward Ray. He spoke clearly and looked right into Ray's eyes. "I'm so glad you could come tonight."

Ray took in his dark suit and crisp white shirt. He looked very gentlemanly. Ray caught herself thinking this might not have been a bad idea after all! She quickly corrected herself; she knew Jake did not have feelings for her and was determined not to get caught up in all of these feelings. She would not get her heart broken. Sarah motioned for them to sit down. Ray and her father took a seat across from Jake and his parents on the couch. Bob cleared his throat and spoke, "Jake, I take it your father has spoken to you of our arrangement?" Jake nodded but did not speak.

Bob continued, "Do you agree to combine the two ranches in marriage?"

Jake looked at Ray for several seconds trying to guess what she was thinking. "If this is the best way to guarantee the ranches stay in our two families, then I agree. How does Ray feel about it?" Jake looked back to Ray waiting for an answer.

Ray looked at Jake and raised her chin. "If this is the best way to combine the two ranches, then I will do my part to keep them together. I agree."

Jake nodded and searched Ray's face for anything that would give him an idea of how she really felt. Ray had always been stubborn and prided herself on doing things her own way. Jake was having a hard time believing that she would accept this without a fight. He knew she believed herself capable of running the ranch by herself with the help of Sam. Sarah smiled and said, "If we are all in agreement, we should discuss the arrangements." Sarah turned to Jim, willing him to continue. "We can have the wedding at the church in town. I'm sure the reverend will not have a problem with this. How soon can we get everything in order?"

Ray cleared her throat and spoke up. "We don't have to have the service at a church. We could just go to the justice of the peace and have him marry us."

Sarah looked shocked, "Rayne, honey, you only get married once. Just because this is an arrangement between two families does not mean you're not entitled to a ceremony and everything that goes with it. Please reconsider."

Ray looked at Sarah. Ray had never considered how Jake felt about the ceremony. She turned to Jake. "Jake what do you prefer?

Jake looked first at his mother, and then to Ray, he spoke softly. "Ray, I think we should follow through with this as traditionally as possible. The whole town will be talking of our engagement, and it will be expected of us to have the usual ceremony. After all, the only ones that will know that this has been arranged will be the people in this room. To everyone else, we are a happy couple desperately in love." He gave her a wink as he added the last part. Ray tried to calm herself as she processed everything Jake had said. She looked to her father, but he was smiling smugly.

Ray looked to Sarah again and said, "Mrs. Hale, I believe I was wrong. It will be important to follow through with this as Jake has said. Although I do have to admit that I have no experience whatsoever in this area, so I will be relying on you to help me."

Sarah smiled at Ray. "Of course, honey, and Ray, please call me Sarah. After all, we will be family very soon."

She took a breath and spoke again. "So we have settled on a church ceremony, but we have not talked about when the ceremony will take place."

Jim looked to Sarah and said, "How much time do you need to prepare? Can we have the ceremony in a week?

Sarah considered this and answered, "There should not be a problem getting the license. We should be able to have the wedding at the end of next week." Ray clenched her hands in her skirts and tried to keep the smile in place on her face. A week! Were they out of their minds! She would have to work very hard to convince Jake this was not a good idea. She needed time to speak to him alone.

Jake looked to Ray and said, "Do you agree to the ceremony being at the end of next week. Today being Friday, that gives us seven days to get everything ready."

Ray looked at Jake for several seconds before she answered. Was he really going to go through with this? But why? He was not stressed about his father's ranch. She was sure of that. So why was he rushing this? To make his parents happy? "I'm not sure if that will be enough time. I don't know how long it takes to make a dress. Sarah, do you know a seamstress in town who can make the dress for me?" Sarah nodded, and Ray continued, "Sarah, if you believe there will be enough time, then I will have to accept your opinion. I will be ready by Friday." She turned to Jake again and was surprised at the wide smile on his face. Why was he not upset? He should be mad that all of this is in place and so soon. But instead, he was sitting there like the cat that swallowed the canary! He rose and excused himself. Sarah ushered us into the dining room for supper. Jake returned a few minutes later and took the seat beside Ray. He had a small box in his hands, and he placed it on the table in front of her. Ray swallowed the lump in her throat and reached out to pick up the box.

As she started to open it, Jake cleared his throat and said, "It was my grandmother's. It passes down the line to me. Since you are my bride, it is natural for you to have it." She looked across the table at his mother and was shocked at the tears in her eyes. Was everyone going crazy around here? They acted like it was natural for Jake and Ray to be, she struggled on the word, *engaged!* Jake took the ring from the box and pulled Ray's hand to him. He looked her straight in the eyes and slipped the ring on her finger. Ray gasped at what she saw in his eyes. There were feelings there, feelings that Ray didn't understand. Feelings she didn't want to know he was capable of. She let her eyes drift close and was surprised when a tear slipped down her cheek. Jake wiped his knuckle across her cheek to remove it. She opened her eyes and said the only thing she could, "Thank you, Jake."

Her father cleared his throat and said, "Well, congratulations, Jake. I think you got you a good one. No one will work harder on the ranch than Ray. You two will have a happy life together. I'm sure of it." He held his glass high as he toasted us. It was more than Ray could handle. She excused herself in a rush and ran from the room.

Outside, she sat on the corral fence looking down the hill. She didn't hear Jake approach; he walked up beside her. Leaning on the rail, he nudged her with his shoulder; she huffed and inched over away from him. He just stepped closer and pressed up against her again. They stood there a few minutes in silence before he finally spoke. "Ray, are you sure you're okay with this? You seem very upset. No one is pushing you into this. If you don't want to marry me, you should say so now before it is too late."

She laughed and jumped off the fence. Turning to face him, she put her hands on her hips then said, "Do you really think I have a choice in this? We have hated each other since we were kids. Do you really think it is a good idea for us to get married!"

He motioned for her to come closer. She stepped up; he reached out and pulled her by her shoulders until they were nose to nose. He looked into her eyes and moved his mouth to cover hers. She closed her eyes and stood as still as she could, barely even breathing. He took his time, slowly caressing her lips with his. She moved closer before she knew it and wrapped her arms around his shoulders. Tilting her head to the side, he deepened the kiss. Opening her mouth slightly, she gave him the opening he was waiting for; and he quickly slid his tongue into her mouth. Her fingers moved up his neck and into his hair. He pulled his arm back and wrapped it around her waist, pulling her closer still. When they finally came up for air, he had a grin on his face.

"That kiss is the reason I think this could work. There is no denying we have a spark between us. If we can strengthen our two ranches by uniting and get to explore a relationship with each other, then I say *yes*, I believe we should do this."

She took a breath and spoke quietly, almost a whisper. "Why? You don't even like me?"

He sighed and looked up at her. "If you think that then you don't know me at all. I don't want you to do anything that will make you unhappy, so if you don't want to do this, then say so now."

Ray laughed and shoved at him. "Since when? We have fought tooth and nail since we first laid eyes on each other. You don't care about me."

Jake stepped back. She could see the anger in his face. "I was never mean to you, Ray. You were the one causing us to fight. You never would give me a chance to be your friend."

Ray laughed again. "My friend. You were the one always calling me names and picking on me. Why would I want a snake like you to be my friend?"

Jake was really getting mad. Maybe she had gone too far? Maybe if we fought then he would call the marriage off. She would get what she wanted.

"Well, I'm sorry you feel that way about me, but it makes no difference. You will soon have a snake for a husband, so get used to it."

She huffed and fired back without thinking, "I don't have to marry you. There is someone else courting for me, Jake. You are not my only option."

He stared at her, trying to figure out if she was bluffing. "You're lying. Your father would not make this offer if you were courting someone else."

She laughed again. "You don't know my father. He does not want anyone else to get their hands on our ranch. He wants me to run it but not by myself. I can choose Clay. He would run the ranch with me. The ranch would not really be mine, and he would most likely make changes I would not agree with, but I would be married, and that is what my father wants."

She saw the words rake over Jake, but she had no idea how he would react to them. He was instantly in front of her again. His eyes were locked on hers and flaming with fire. He was very mad at her. She suddenly realized she should not have mentioned Clay's name. "You will not see Clay again. You are engaged to me," he spit the words at her. "And you will behave as my fiancée. We will be married at the end of next week, and you *will* become my wife. There is no changing that, and I would appreciate it if you would not swim so late at night in the pond. I may not be the only one who knows you swim there, and I would hate to have to break Clay's neck for spying on my wife swimming *naked*!" He knew he hit home with that one.

She took a large breath and held it in puffing up her chest and making her breasts strain against the low neck of the dress. She shoved him back and yelled at him, "You have been spying on me in the pond? How many times Jake? Did you like what you saw? Is this why my father has suddenly got the idea for us to marry?" Before he could attempt to answer, she shoved on. "Okay, Jake, I will go along with this. But it is only because I will not hurt my father. I will be your wife but only in name. I do not love you, and I never will, and I don't care if you watch me as I swim in the pond. You better get a good look because it will be the only time you will see me without clothes on. Do you understand me?"

Jake took a step back from her taking in her anger and hurt. He should not have told her about the pond. That was a very big mistake. Now he had hurt her, and she would not easily forgive that. "Now, Ray, don't be hasty. I know you have feelings for me. There is no way you could kiss me like you did and not have feelings for me."

Another mistake. She smiled and spit through her teeth. "You were the one who kissed me. I did not kiss you back. I do not have feelings for you. How could I have feelings for someone like you? You are a snake, Jake, and nothing more!" She saw how these words affected him and decided she had made a mistake. As the slow smile crossed his face, he reached out and grabbed her, pulling her roughly up against him.

"We'll see!" he said before he crushed his mouth on hers. She was shocked at how angry he was. His lips were hard on hers. Angry.

She tried to push at his chest, but he wasn't budging. He pulled her to him even more. Her hands trapped between them. He wrapped one of his arms around her, freeing his hand to pull her head back. She felt his tongue hot on her lips urging her to open for him. She wouldn't. She wouldn't. She did. As soon as her lips relaxed, he pushed her mouth open and explored her. She couldn't resist. His lips had turned from hard to soft, and his hands were now caressing her back and neck. He grabbed a handful of her hair shaking the pins out. It cascaded down her back like a waterfall. He wound it up in his hand and sighed; he couldn't help himself. He pulled her into him; she fit so perfectly. All he could think about was her, and he knew he was the only thing on her mind. He slowed his mouth and started to pull away. He heard the small sigh of protest from her lips and smiled. She would not face him. She hid her face in his chest. He heard her whisper "Damn you" and knew he had won. He smiled to himself again and thought it would not be hard being married to Ray at all. It might just be very interesting!

CHAPTER 7

Ray went upstairs and took off her dress. She was exhausted, both mentally and physically. After Jake had let her go, she had hung her head and went back inside. Jake followed her and took his place again beside her. She didn't look at him or make any attempt at conversation; they both ate in silence staying out of the conversation of their parents. When they had finished, she was glad her father seemed to take the hint and suggest they leave. Sarah, Jake's mother, had told Ray she would come over the next day and pick her up. They would need to go to town and see the seamstress. She would have to have plenty of time to get Ray's measurements to start the dress. Ray sat on the side of the bed removing her boots. She removed her dress and sat in her dressing gown. She thought about riding down to the pond but instantly remembered Jake's confession that he had watched her. Oh, well! So he watched her. She was almost convinced he wouldn't be able to see anything. After all, it was dark. Only the moonlight to see by, and it was full of shadows. Would he be expecting me to come tonight? Or did he think I would stay home afraid to see if he had been telling the truth. She walked to her dresser and opened the drawer then opened all the drawers one by one. She stood very still for a moment.

Emma had been busy while she was away. All her mother's dresses that had been put away were now laid out in her drawers. Only one drawer still held her old riding shirts and pants. She picked a thick cotton dress out of the drawer and pulled it over her head. She grabbed a blanket as she walked downstairs. He would not keep her from her pond! She rode up to the tree alongside the pond and slid off her horse and pulled the dress over her head. She laid the blanket and her clothes on the tree limb like always and walked slowly into the water. Once she had reached the point where the water was slightly above her breasts, she said "I hope you are enjoying the view, Jake!" and laughed to herself.

Two words cut her laugh short. "Very much," the low voice she heard was to her left in the shadows of the moonlight. Jake laughed at her startled expression. He slowly moved into the dim light, and Ray could see the smile on his face.

"Don't you come near me!" she said as a shiver of fear ran down her spine. How could she be so stupid? So sure of herself that she wouldn't have noticed Jake in the water. He would have no doubt got a clear view of her as she so brazenly waded into the water. Her cheeks turned crimson in the moonlight. "Why, Ray, if I didn't know you better, I would say you were scared of me." Jake's low voice taunted her.

"I'm not scared of you, Jake. I'm just very annoyed that you are here." Ray responded lifting her chin. "Well If I annoy you so bad why don't you make me leave." He told her as he moved even closer to her. She started backing up. "Jake, you know this is not right. You should not be in here with me like this. We are not married yet." Trying to play the innocent little lady card was not her style, but she was out of options. Jake chuckled to himself; she was really something! But she had come here tonight knowing he would be here. She made her decision, and he was going to hold her to it.

"Don't worry, my bride," he added with a grin. "I will not take your innocence tonight. I will save that for our wedding night. But there is no reason why I cannot get a closer look at your beautiful body." He drifted closer to her. She automatically put her arms over her breasts as to shield herself from his eyes. He was close enough he could grab her now. He saw the realization spread across her face. He reached his hand out as to touch her and heard her gasp of breath. Before she knew what had happened, he had slapped a handful of water into her face. She froze and then started laughing. He laughed as well. She removed her hand and slapped water at him in return. Soon, they had a water fight going, and her shyness with him was forgotten. She dove into the water and tried to pull him under. He was stronger than her and quickly dunked her instead. She came up behind him and jumped on his back, trying to use her weight to push him under. He grabbed her arms and pulled her over his head. When she came up, she was facing him. She was gasping for air and trying to laugh at the same time. She was holding onto his arms. She realized a second to late that her body was rubbing up against his. As she looked up at him, she saw the seriousness in his face. The rippling of the water from their fight broke against his chest. She could easily see the muscles rolling in his arms and the taught skin over muscle spread across his dark hair spattered chest. She took a breath to steady herself and brushed her hand over the hair on his chest. Her heart was running a race she was about to lose. She looked back up into his eyes, leaving her hand on his chest. She could see the emotion in his eyes and knew he was reacting to her closeness the same way. She could hear his labored breathing and feel the heat from his body slowly warming hers. She rubbed her hand through the hair on his chest again, slowly raising her hand to explore the muscles in his arms. He flexed his muscles under her light fingers, making her smile. She couldn't bear this anymore. She moved closer to him, winding their legs together; she sighed deeply and laid her face into his chest. He wrapped his arms around her and kissed the top of her head. "It's not supposed to be like this between us. How could it change so much? We are supposed to hate each other. Now we can't keep our hands off each other. Why is it so different?" She choked out in a strangled voice.

He laughed softly. "Ray, we have grown up. We have changed over the years and are looking for something different, something we both want, something we can give each other."

She sighed again and pushed herself into him more, shielding her face from him. "I don't know how to be a wife, Jake. I don't know how to cook, sow, or keep house. I have always done the chores, branded the cattle, and broke the horses. I don't know how to be a lady, and I don't want to be one," she added softly.

He tried to keep from laughing. "You know, I met lots of ladies in the city, but I knew I would never marry any of them. Do you know why?"

She thought about this for a minute. "No," she whispered.

41

He smiled again. "Because I was not looking for a flower that would wilt and die. I was looking for a strong tree that will stand tall beside me. Do you understand me, Ray?"

She thought about this for a minute. "Are you calling me a tree?" she said, trying to hide her smile.

"I guess I am," he said. "Why do you want *me*, Jake? There has to be more trees out there." She smiled as she continued with his analogy. "Ones with pretty flowers that bloom in spring."

Jake thought about this for a minute. "I guess because I've never seen one bloom as fast as you have. One day you were a puny little bush, and the next thing I knew, you were a tall sturdy tree in full bloom. I couldn't turn away. At first, I thought I could just look at you and be able to admire the beauty you have become, but I soon realized that I couldn't walk away. I had to have the whole tree for myself."

She was still for a few minutes before she answered, "I guess I should be flattered that you're calling me pretty, but could you stop comparing me to a tree!" She laughed and shoved at him. Jake splashed water at her in return and laughed. "What are we going to do?" she asked, still splashing water.

"We're going to get married at the end of the week, and everything is going to be right as rain!" They both laughed and started swimming toward the bank. When they realized what they were doing, Jake spoke. "You can get out first. I will turn my back. I'll get out after you leave."

Ray looked at him wide eyed. Had he already forgotten what happened years ago when he was stuck in the pond naked? "Are you sure you trust me to get only my clothes?" she teased him.

Jake smiled and swam closer to the bank. "This time, I will not hesitate to chase you down and whoop your tail. Fiancée or not!"

Ray smiled wider. "Are you sure you could catch me? After all, you would be riding your horse without a stitch of clothing on. I'm sure you will be pretty sore by the time you catch me." Jake nodded his head agreeing with her.

"Well, I don't *have* to turn my back while you get out. We could get out together. I was not joking about taking a look at your beautiful body."

Ray cleared her throat as sudden heat flushed her cheeks. "Okay, you win. I will not mess with your clothes. I promise." Jake nodded his head again. She motioned for him to turn his back. Jake spun in the water and faced the opposite side of the pond. He could hear her walking out of the water. He could imagine her drying off with the blanket she had brought. It was only too easy to think of that soft cotton dress as she pulled it over her shoulders and down around the smooth curves of her skin. "Okay," she called when she had dressed and mounted her horse. Jake turned around and smiled. "Don't forget. My mother is coming to take you to town tomorrow. Honey," he added with a grin.

"I will not forget, Jake." And as she started to turn, she threw over her shoulder "and don't call me honey!" He laughed out loud and started swimming toward the bank. Ray turned her horse toward home and took off.

Jake stood and walked toward the pine trees that shielded the pond from his house. He reached the tree where he hung his clothes and started drying off. He rode home feeling light in the saddle. He was happy. Ray had responded to him like he had never expected. She may be full of fire, stubborn, and definitely a tomboy, but she had showed him a side of her that was passionate and sweet. It warmed him to think about the way he felt about her. He was dangerously close to loving her. One question she had asked kept playing over and over again in his mind. How could the way they felt for each other change so much? He thought about the answer to that question again. He had told her that they had grown up, but what if he was wrong? They were both content with the life of a rancher. Neither had ever dreamed of leaving Odessa, Texas, and never would. They both cared a great deal for their parents. So why was a match between them so crazy? He could not think of anyone she would be better suited with than him. Clay's face drifted into his mind. He was instantly angry. *I'll be damned*, he thought to himself. Rayne Whitmore would not be marring anyone but him. He was the only one who could really appreciate her for who she was. He was sure of that!

CHAPTER 8

Ray woke early and wandered downstairs. She started making coffee, the only thing close to cooking that she had been able to master. She hoped her future husband liked coffee. Lots and lots of coffee. Emma had offered to give her more lessons. Trying to teach her the basics, she told Ray that the rest would come if she got the basics; however, she was a little scared to try again after what had happened before. Emma seemed a little scared too, but she knew Emma would never admit it. She poured herself a cup and set down at the table. It had been two days since they had gotten engaged. Sarah had come and took her to town. She had commissioned a whole wardrobe instead of just a wedding dress. When Ray had tried to talk her out of it, she had said, "Well, honey, you will need more than this one dress. Your mother's dresses are very beautiful and special to you, but they were not made for you. They do not fit you as they should."

Ray had smiled and let her have her way. Sarah was a sweet woman. She had tried to calm Ray's mind by telling her about her and Jim's arranged marriage. Ray had never known that Sarah did not marry Jim out of love but because of an arrangement between their families. Sarah looked at Jim with so much emotion in her eyes. Sarah had explained how she was scared at first, but after she and Jim had married and she had discovered his gentle, caring nature, she had fallen deeply in love with him so much so that she could not imagine another person that matched her so well. She was absolutely sure that her parents had made an excellent choice for her husband. How could I be so sure? She had not felt comfortable talking about her emotions with Sarah. She had a warm smile and encouraged Ray to tell her how she was feeling, but would Sarah not protect her own son if Ray got out of line with her feelings toward Jake? Sarah had said for her to think of her as a mother, but she was so used to not having one all these years.

It was hard to open up to anyone besides Emma. She couldn't even talk to her father about these things. Ray had done a lot of thinking over these last few days. She had come to the conclusion that Jake obviously had no intentions of backing out, and she would not either; however, she had no intention of simply assuming the role of the *good wife*. Sarah had said that a marriage was a partnership. Well, Jake and she would have a partnership, nothing physical. Simply a good friendship. She was not ready or willing to lay her heart out to him, especially since she had no idea whether he would cherish it or rip it to pieces and toss it back to her. Jake had definitely made it clear he wanted her, but he had never claimed to love her. She would not easily give herself to someone who had not proven they truly deserved her. After all, marriage was forever, or at least as long as one of you were still breathing. If he pushed his luck on their wedding night, the marriage would be over quick. She smiled to herself at that thought. She was not stupid enough to imagine that Jake will agree with her. Not without a fight anyway. She had not seen him since that night at the pond. She wondered what he had been up to. She knew he was running the ranch, but he had lots of hands to do most of the work. He would more or less just have to supervise.

She sat wondering what he looked like as he worked. His work shirt pulled tight over his bulging muscles as he lifted posts for the fence. She tipped her chair back on two legs and let her mind wander, imagining he would be soaked with sweat in the heat of July in Texas. He would need to cool off after a hard day's work. She thought of the pond and how he looked with his hair wet and black, falling into his eyes in thick locks. His fierce green eyes smoldering as he looked down at her. She remembered how his eyes had held her in a trance just before he had kissed her the first time. How they had smoked with fury when his face had been covered with flour and how they had looked a shimmering emerald green when she had rubbed her body up against his so full of passion and desire. His body had been a hard mass of muscle as he held himself rigid for her appraisal. All those muscles in all the right places under his soft tan skin. His stomach was so flat and hard; the soft black hair scattered across his chest. She licked her lips, so engrossed in her thoughts she missed Sam walking into the kitchen. She was completely ignoring him, and he didn't like it.

Suddenly, Ray flopped backward into the floor. She jumped up in a whirl of cuss words as she tried to understand how her chair had tipped backward far enough to dump her out of it. Sam's laughter quickly answered that question. She turned a killer look on him. He held up his hands in surrender and quickly said, "Hey, don't look at me that way. You were completely out of it. I said your name twice." He grinned as she looked stunned. "You can daydream about your future husband later. We've got cows to brand." Sam turned and walked out of the house, still laughing. Ray took another minute to compose herself; maybe the embarrassment would be out of her face before she had to go in front of the other hands. *Gosh*, she thought, *I really got carried away there! Best to keep my thoughts away from Jake for now. Don't want to fall of my horse and make an even bigger fool of myself.*

She would wait to think of him when she was alone in her room, much safer there. She grabbed her hat hanging by the back door and walked out to the barn to get her horse. She had a long day; the sooner she got started, the sooner it would be over. She didn't like the chore of branding cows too well. They were slippery little things. If you didn't catch them just right, they would quickly slip out of the rope and be gone before you could blink. She saddled her horse and rode out to join the rest of the guys.

They greeted her as usual. They all liked her as far as she knew. She had never had words with one of them. She wasn't sure who they were scared of more—her, her father, or Sam. She guessed she never would. Sam cleared his throat again catching her attention. "Guess you'll be busy today." His simple comment caught her off guard. She looked at him, startled by his words. He tipped his hat in the direction behind her. She turned to look behind her and cussed under her breath.

Think of the man, and here he comes barreling down the road to her house looking all hot and bothered. *Well, I wonder what he's up to now*, she thought. She turned her horse toward him and called for Sam and the others to go on without her. As she met up with Jake, she discovered he had a smile on his face.

"Well hello, honey," he said as he walked his horse up to hers.

She rolled her eyes and asked, "What are you doing here, Jake? I'm sure you have something better to do like run a ranch. I sure do."

Jake grinned again. "Well, I sure do, but I thought I would take a minute to tell you about our plans tonight."

Our plans, she thought. This man has lost it.

"Why do you think *we* have plans tonight? Do you have a frog in your pocket, Jake?" she said laughing.

Jake looked at her with another dazzling grin. "No, I don't have a frog in my pocket, but you better have some dancing shoes."

She looked at him with wide eyes. "Jake, I'm not going dancing with you. I don't dance, and even if I did, it wouldn't be with you."

Jake cleared his throat and said, "Well, you know, the church has been raising money with bake sales and such. Well, I guess they thought since they raised all the money they needed they would reward the town with a little dance. Nothing fancy," he said, raising his hands. "You don't have to get all gussied up. I would like you to wear a dress, but you don't have to go all out."

Ray took a deep breath and spoke slowly. "Jake, I don't do dances. I have some dresses, but they're old, and I don't like wearing them much. They don't fit well." She looked at him and saw him smiling.

"Well, we're lucky. The seamstress came to see Mom yesterday. She left a couple dresses she had adjusted to fit your measurements, and Mom is coming over here this evening to help you get ready. Don't hate me, Ray. It's just one night. Everyone is expecting us to go. We are engaged you know, and this is expected of us."

Ray took another deep breath to steady herself. He was so tricky. He knew I would have to agree if he played the everyone-is-expecting-us-to card, and it definitely didn't help that his mother was already coming over. "Okay, Jake, but don't whine when I step on your feet. I warned you."

He grinned and said, "I'll be here to get you at six. Mom is coming about five." He tipped his hat, and as he turned to leave, he said, "See you then, honey." Ray rolled her eyes and turned her horse toward the pasture. She would have to hurry to get all her work done and get back to the house in time to wash up before his mom arrived.

When they had finished the last calf, she stood and dusted her pants off. She looked a mess. She had mud caked up on the knees of her pants, on her shirt, and she was sure there were smudges of it on her face. She was soaked with sweat, and her clothes were sticking to her like a second skin. She said bye to the guys and headed to the house. She would have to soak in the tub for hours to get this smell out. Emma had already started heating the water for her bath. Ah, she was the best woman in the world. She walked by Emma and sat down to take her boots off.

"Emma? Do you think I'm crazy for letting Jake talk me into this?" she said.

"Not at all, honey. All you do is work, work, work all day long. You need some time to enjoy yourself," she said shaking her head. "But I don't see how I can enjoy myself with Jake there."

Emma turned to look at her. "Well, you better get used to it. In a few days, he will be your husband. You will be all alone in that house with him. What you going to do, ride home to your daddy?"

Ray listened but could not comprehend Emma's words. "What do you mean in that house?"

Emma looked as if she was confused. "Where do you think the two of you will live? Not here and not with his parents. You will have your own house. It is only proper for a couple to start their own lives in their own house." She looked like she was about to laugh. This had never crossed Ray's mind. Why couldn't they just live like they do now? Why did they have to live together? Surely, they would not expect her to live in a house alone with Jake and sleep in the same bed as him. Oh, God, they did. What was she going to do?

She immediately thought of Jake's comment at the pond the other night. "I will save that for the wedding night." Oh, she was close to passing out. She swallowed the lump in her throat. Emma

48

must have noticed her anxiety at what she had just said. She crossed the room to Ray and put her hand on her shoulder.

"Ray, honey, are you okay?" Ray looked up at Emma's stunned face, but no words would come. "Ray, calm down. Did you not realize what would happen on you wedding night?" Ray was sure she turned at least three shades of red.

She tried to speak again slowly. "I…can't" was all she could choke out.

"Well, you're going to have to." Emma stared back at Ray. "Honey, did your mama ever tell you what happens between a man and a woman when they get married?" Ray looked away. Surely, this was not happening. They were not discussing what was going to happen when Jake got her home on their wedding night, not only because it was embarrassing but because it was not going to happen.

"Yes, I know what is supposed to happen, but that is not going to happen. I'm only marrying Jake because I have to. I don't love him. I can't do that with him."

Emma looked at her with a puzzled expression. After a minute, she said, "Ray, you think about that man all the time. That kiss you two had was not something you would do with someone you don't like." She waited for Ray to respond before she asked, "How do you feel when you're around him?"

Because she loved Emma and would not hurt her feelings, she answered honestly, "Like I've got a hive of bees in my stomach. I can't think I can only feel the bees stinging me, like they're stinging me all over, kind of tingly."

Emma smiled as she looked at Ray. Oh boy, this girl didn't know anything about love. She couldn't really be surprised the only affection she had ever gotten was from her father and Emma. She had never had a boy swoon over her. Emma sighed, "Ray, you should really look at Jake tonight. Think about how he makes you feel. Let him show you how he feels. Give him time to talk and listen to what he is trying to tell you. You may just find that he has some strong feelings for you."

Ray looked at Emma with a grin. "Okay, Emma, whatever you say."

Ray turned and headed upstairs to the bathtub; she couldn't think of anything but the dreaded wedding night. She was thinking seriously about drowning herself in the tub. She was sure no one would miss her, except maybe Jake, only because he couldn't wait to get his hands on her. Oh, he would definitely get the surprise of his life on his wedding night. He better get extra blankets because she was not going to be the one warming his bed at night.

CHAPTER 9

Jake set in Ray's dining room waiting with her father. His mother had been here an hour already, and she was still not done. Jake was starting to get nervous. He wondered if Ray had jumped out the window and his mother was trying to catch her. He smiled at that thought. Bob cleared his throat and nodded to signal someone was coming down the stairs. Emma came into the room. Jake's mother stepped off the steps into the dining room. She had a wide smile on her face. She turned to look up the stairs and called to Ray, "Come on down here."

Jake walked to the bottom of the steps and waited for Ray to come down. After a few minutes, he hollered up to her, "You know, I'll come up there and get you. Better to come down yourself." He heard the creaking of the floor as she walked to the top of the stairs. Jake stood frozen in place looking up at the gorgeous beauty staring down at him. He couldn't look away. He followed her every step, every movement, and swish of her dress as she took a step.

She was wearing a light blue silk dress cut low in the front with a ruffle of lace to cover the swelling of her breast. She wore a petticoat under the dress, and as she pulled her dress up in the front to come down the steps, he could easily see the thick layers making the dress fluff out from the curve of her waist. She wore white leather riding boots with lace up the sides. Her auburn hair was twisted back from her face and hanging down her back, and on top of her head was a light blue hat tipped forward to shield her gorgeous face from sun. The pale blue of the dress set of the cream of her skin and those gorgeous freckles across her nose and cheeks.

When she got to the bottom step, he moved back to give her a little room. His eyes never left hers. Her ice blue eyes stared straight back at him trying to judge his reaction. Emma blew her nose drawing everyone's attention to her. She stood with a handkerchief to her nose, tears spilling down her face. Ray's father quickly stepped to her and put his arm around her shoulder. He leaned in and whispered something in her ear. She nodded and tried to calm herself.

Ray looked back at Jake and was surprised when he held his hand out to her. She laid her delicate gloved hand in his. He pulled it up to his lips, and still looking in her eyes, he kissed it very softly— just a whisper of lips on her soft skin. Her pink lips turned up in a smile. Jake turned to his mother with a smile and gave her a wink. He turned back to Ray and asked, "Are you ready to go?"

She replied in a small voice, "Sure, maybe everyone else will not stare so much." She shot a smoldering look at her father. Surely, he knew how uncomfortable this made her.

Jake smiled and said, "I doubt it. No one has ever seen anything so lovely in Texas. All of the men will be green with jealousy. I will have to watch you carefully, honey." He led her to the door and out to the wagon before she had a chance to change her mind. He lifted her easily into the buggy. With a tip of his hat toward her father, he climbed into the buggy and slapped the reins, steering the horses toward town. Ray sat quietly beside him.

She was still reeling at his reaction when they got close to town. She stole a look at Jake and was happy he didn't catch her. She had been too worried about his reaction to her that she had not paid attention to his clothes. He was wearing a black Western suit with a white shirt and vest; he wore a bowtie at his neck. She giggled to herself. A bowtie, how gentlemanly. She would bet they looked a sight in the middle of Texas dressed like they were going to a party in the city.

She was distracted by the way his muscles moved under the thin fabric of his dinner jacket. His arms were midsize and roped in muscle. His chest was wide and thick with muscle as well. His stomach was flat and curved into his waist. She would not allow herself the think of anything below his waist. She was still upset about that whole wedding night thing. Better to take care of this before the big part, she figured.

She cleared her throat, drawing Jake's attention to her. "Jake, I need to talk to you about something." Jake nodded to her and urged her to go on. She fiddled with her skirt and looked at her hands. "Where are we going to live after we get married?"

He grinned. "Don't worry about that, honey. Me and the boys are working daylight to dark to get the house finished before the wedding."

Ray tried to keep the shock out of her voice, "Is there going to be more than one bed?"

Jake laughed. "Why would we need another bed right now? Last time I checked, it takes nine months before a baby is born."

Ray gasped at his words. "You can't mean that we will have to sleep in the same bed? Jake, I barely know you."

He tried to keep his voice light. "There will be plenty of time for us to get to know each other. Don't worry," he added.

Ray took a deep breath before she answered, "Jake, I can't sleep with you."

Jake looked at her again trying to keep the grin from his face. "Do you snore?"

Ray punched him playfully on the arm. "Don't be funny, Jake. I am serious. You've been back in town all of what, a month? We're getting married, and I don't even know you?" She looked at him with pleading eyes.

Jake thought about what she was saying. "Ray, are you scared?" She was silent for a few minutes. He wondered if she would give him an answer. "You don't need to be scared of me. I would never hurt you, Ray." She looked up at him with fear in her face. He knew she had never done anything past kissing a boy, and that one experience had been with him. He was sure he could convince her he would be gentle with her, but would she agree to the consummation of their marriage?

Did she know they were not married until they had shared their souls? Her mother had died when she was just a girl, but the passion she had showed him in their kiss and when they had swum together told him she was not completely unaware of what happened between a man and a woman. He knew she was capable of loving. He had never considered she would be afraid of this. He was certain she would not submit to it easily, but afraid? He had thought she was not afraid of anything. It looked like she had been holding out on him.

Ray squirmed on the bench next to him, anxious to arrive at the dance and be rid of this horrible feeling she had. She had just told Jake she was afraid. She would never live this down. She was not supposed to be afraid of anything even though she had never done anything like this before. The only contact she had ever had with a boy was just a few days ago when she had kissed Jake. He definitely had an effect on her. She could still remember the feel of her skin sliding against his in the water. She had no trouble recalling the images of his tan body in the moonlight. Hadn't she got into trouble thinking about him that very morning?

She decided she was not going to discuss this anymore. She would deal with it when she had to. She was determined to follow Emma's advice and enjoy herself. She had set through all the torture Jake's mother had put her through. She was not going to waste her efforts.

Jake pulled up in front of the barn the town used for dances and other parties. Jake jumped down and came around to help Ray from the buggy. She started to jump down herself but changed her mind. She didn't want to take a chance on ripping her dress. Sarah had gone to so much trouble. She would take care of the gifts she had been given. Jake put his hands around her waist and lifted her effortlessly from the buggy. She had put her hands on his shoulders to steady herself. She looked up into his face and saw him smiling. She instantly smiled in return before she realized what she was doing.

Jake took her hand and walked her around the horses toward the barn. She stepped close to him. He smelled nice. She inhaled his tangy fragrance. It was very masculine just what she would have imagined him wearing. He looked down at her and smiled again. "Ready?" he said as he stopped at the door.

"Yes," she said smiling into his face. Jake pushed the door open, and they stepped inside.

There were groups of chatting people scattered around the walls. Someone had swept the hay from the floor leaving a large space for dancing. A band had been set up in one corner. Mr. Baker was serving punch at one of the tables filled with drinks. Another table was next to it with all kinds of dishes heaped with food. Jake asked her if she was thirsty, and she nodded no. She kept looking around the room at all the faces staring back at her. She blushed and turned her face into Jake's arm. "Hey," he whispered, "They'll stop soon. It's not every day they get to see the prettiest girl in Texas in a dress."

She looked up at him and saw a sweet smile on his face. He was trying to calm her to make her feel better; she squeezed his arm and straightened up. They walked over to the punch table. Mr. Baker looked up with a question on his lips. It died the instant his eyes touched Ray's face. A slow smile grew wide on his face. "Ray, ah," he sighed, "such a beauty you have become. Jake, you are very lucky man to get such a beautiful bride."

Ray looked up at Jake. He looked into her clear eyes as he spoke to Mr. Baker. "Thank you, Mr. Baker, I certainly think so."

Ray blushed and looked back at Mr. Baker. "Was Mrs. Elsa able to come tonight?"

Mr. Baker smiled wide again. "Why, yes, she is over there taking it easy. She must get plenty of rest if she is going to get better." Ray looked at Mr. Baker with sympathy in her eyes. He loved his wife so much. She wondered if she would ever think of Jake like that.

"We will go visit her then. See you later, Mr. Baker." Jake turned her, and they started across the dance floor toward Mrs. Baker. The band had just started playing a slow little waltz. Jake looked down to Ray. "Would you like to dance?" Ray looked a little bit startled. They had come to a dance after all.

"Not right now, but thank you." She smiled at him. It was starting to get easier to be nice to him, especially when he looked at her with that dazzling smile with her hand on his arm and smelling so wonderful. They reached the side of the dance floor where Mrs. Baker was sitting, a blanket covering her legs.

Ray took a seat beside her and started talking to her. Jake excused himself to talk to some of the other men. Ray was quickly caught up in a discussion with Mrs. Baker. Neither one of them noticed the cocky rancher that walked through the door.

CHAPTER 10

Jake positioned himself across the room from Ray, so he would be able to keep an eye on her, but soon, the men crowded around; and he lost sight of her. He was getting annoyed answering questions about how he was able to tame the wild Rayne. Why couldn't anyone just accept her for the beauty she was and leave it at that? Charlie, one of his friends from Philadelphia, would not be giving him so much grief over his chosen bride. He was fairly sure of that.

The men around him started to turn to the dance floor. Something had caught their attention. Jake stepped around one of them to get a look himself. He froze where he was and felt like the floor fell out from under him. He blinked several times trying to clear the image from his eyes. It could not be his Rayne being twirled on the dance floor by no one other than Clay Elliot.

Jake's hands flexed into fists at his side. He was talking to her, and she was nodding at him. She looked out across the floor nervously like she was afraid of getting caught. Well, she should be. Jake stepped out of the crowd and started toward her. He had almost reached them when Clay spun her in his arms bending her backward and kissing her. Jake could hear the shocked gasps of the crowd watching them. When Clay rose back up, he met Jake's angry gaze.

He cleared his throat and grinned. "Just giving her congratulations, Jake. No hard feelings. Right?" Jake didn't even register the shock on Ray's face as she took in his brutal gaze and the way his body was shaking with anger. Before she could say anything, Jake pulled his arm up behind him and took a swing at Clay. Clay had no idea what was coming. He was completely defenseless. Jake's fist caught him square on the nose. There was a loud pop, and his nose started gushing blood.

Ray gasped and tried to help Clay. She hollered for someone to bring her a rag. Before she could hand it to Clay, Jake grabbed her arm and started hauling her out of the barn. She screamed and kicked, but she was no match for his strength. Jake didn't slow as he reached the doors. One kick had the door swinging open and out of his way. He dragged Ray out to the side of the barn. He pushed her up against the wall and put his hands on either side of her to hold her there.

Jake was standing in front of her breathing fast and still shaking with anger. She started to speak but thought better of it. She gave him a few minutes to calm down. After what she saw on the dance floor she sure wasn't going to go around with him. After a few minutes, his breathing started to slow. He spoke softly, almost a whisper, but you could still hear the pure rage in his voice. "What the hell were you doing in there?" He didn't even pause to let her answer. "Did I not tell you that you would not see him again?"

Ray's jaw instantly tightened. Surely, he was not accusing her of anything but dancing with Clay? She kept her teeth clenched and spoke. "You insisted I come to this stupid dance. You should of thought about Clay being here."

He raised his eyes and looked at her then. "Well, I did think about him being here, but I assumed you wouldn't have anything to do with him. I guess I was wrong. I never would have guessed you would have been hanging all over him or so eager to have his mouth on yours."

She huffed and pushed him back. He didn't budge and inch. "You're so full of yourself. I wasn't hanging on him, and I sure as hell didn't want his mouth on mine. You left me to go talk to your friends. What was I supposed to do?" She looked up into his face, her eyes hard.

He leaned even closer to her. "I expected you to say *no*! You sure don't have a problem telling me *no*!" He snapped at her.

She raised her chin before she spoke, looking him in the eyes. "You're absolutely right, Jake. I don't have a problem telling you no. Listen carefully, I will not marry you Friday. I could not imagine

being married to a jealous, hot headed SOB like you. It's over, Jake."
She pushed past him and started walking back toward the barn door.

Jake quickly caught up with her and turned her around to face
him. "We are getting married on Friday, and that is the end of it!"
His eyes were full of the fury he was feeling.

"Jake, it is over. We never should have started this. You obviously don't care about me enough to trust me. I won't live like that.
It's over, Jake. Maybe if you could try controlling your temper long
enough to get the facts straight, someone might be able to care for
you, but it sure won't be me!" She snapped back at him. She turned
again and walked into the barn. She walked right up to Clay, ignoring his shocked expression. "Will you please take me home?" She
looked up at him, waiting for his response. "Sure," he said after a few
seconds.

She turned and headed back toward the door. They walked
out to Clay's wagon. Jake was still standing beside the barn. If looks
could kill, Clay and Ray would have died instantly. *Oh, well, let's see
how he likes this,* she thought. *He wants to accuse me of wanting Clay's
affection? I'll show him.* With a determined set of her jaw, she climbed
into the buggy. Clay took his seat beside her. With a quick slap of
the reins, the horses started out onto the road. She risked one more
look at Jake. He was standing by the barn with his head in his hands.

She couldn't explain what that did to her; she could see the rigid
line of his shoulders as he turned to walk to his wagon. She wondered
if he would come after her and found herself hoping he would. She
had been so consumed with how gorgeous he looked tonight and the
way he made her feel. He had looked at her like she was his sun. She
couldn't have asked for him to behave better at first. He stayed right
beside her, giving her support in more ways than one. She had kept
her arm firmly in his, loving the feel of his muscles moving under
her fingers.

How could she deny that when she looked at him, her heart
missed a beat, but admitting that made her hurt even worse. She had
believed their fairytale would come true until Clay had entered the
room. Was he jealous? She had accused him of it, and he didn't deny
it. Was that what made him see red with anger and not take a few

minutes to really see the situation for what it was? She couldn't care less about Clay's nose. He deserved what he got. She was going to do the same thing, but Jake beat her to it. He should have known better than to kiss her.

She looked over at him in the wagon. He had a sad look on his face. He reached his hand out and wiped the side of her face. She was very still. It took her a few seconds to realize what he was doing. She had obviously been crying, and he was wiping one of the tears from her face. Why was she crying? Because she was thinking about Jake? She was not used to being so emotional. She looked away from him, hoping the wind would dry her face. She didn't like the feel of his hands against her skin. They were not soft and gentle like Jake's had once been.

They pulled up in front of her house. Clay jumped down from the wagon and turned to help her down. She brushed his hands away and jumped down herself. He cleared his throat and said, "Ray, I'm truly sorry about what happened tonight. I had no idea Jake had such a temper. I'm sorry. I hope he didn't hurt you." Ray looked up at him. He was not grinning, but she could hear the amusement in his words. He cleared his throat and spoke again. "Ray, I was wondering. Since you're not marrying Jake now, will you consider courting me again? I know we had some problems the first time around, but I will do everything I know how to make sure you have a good time."

She blinked and took a few seconds to answer. "Well, thank you for thinking of me, but I won't be courting anyone anymore. I don't have feelings for anyone. I am happier by myself." He looked mad when she looked up at him, but he quickly concealed it. He had a smile on his face as he turned to leave. She turned toward the porch and walked up to sit in the rocking chair. She watched Clay's back as he went up the road. What did he have to smile about? She had just told him she didn't have feelings for him. Why would he smile?

She sat, thinking about that for a few more minutes. She could hear Jake's wagon coming up the road. Would he come to see if she made it home okay? She wondered how he was feeling now and what he was thinking. If he would accept defeat and tell his parents the wedding was off or would he keep trying to convince her to marry him? She secretly hoped it was the last. She held her breath when she heard him stop the horses at the entrance to their ranch. It was several seconds before she heard the slap of the reins driving the horses on. So he didn't want to see her tonight, possibly ever again. A fresh set of tears fell down her face at the thought of not seeing Jake again.

She rushed up to her room and took her dress off. She jerked her dresser drawer open and grabbed a shirt and a pair of pants. She threw them on and rushed downstairs. The house was quiet, so her father must be in the bed. She didn't slow as she reached the backdoor. She stalked to the barn and mounted her horse. She didn't waste time saddling him, quickly fashioning a rope halter to him, and riding out bareback straight to the pond secretly hoping Jake would be there. Maybe if they could talk alone, they could talk about what had really happened.

She sat on the side of the pond throwing stones into the black water. The night grew darker at first then lighter as it was getting morning. Jake never showed. She had never cried so much in her life. With every lonely minute that passed, her body shook with sobs for the man she knew would not come. She had made it clear to him she didn't want him, and just like the stubborn man he was, he would not come here to see if she was telling the truth. This had been their place. They had played, aggravated, and once loved here, but now there was nothing but the empty silence and the beating of her broken heart. Close to morning, she rode her horse back home and put him back in the barn. She climbed the stairs slowly. When she reached her bed, she collapsed into the covers and finally free of the tears that wanted to flow, she slept.

CHAPTER 11

Jake sat at the kitchen table, drinking his coffee, running the images from last night over again in his head. He was trying to understand how everything had gotten so messed up. He and Ray had been fine until that snake Clay had walked in. She was sitting with Mrs. Baker, talking with a smile on her face. He was answering questions and trying to make up a good excuse to get her to dance with him. He had gotten distracted by one of the ranch hand's questions. Before he knew what was going on, he had punched Clay and broke his nose then pulled Ray outside and was lashing into her. He knew she had feelings for him, but why was she dancing with Clay?

She could have said no, but he knew that would have made her look rude in front of Mrs. Baker. If she'd have known how he would react, would she have said no or take her chances anyway? He had intended on getting some answers last night, but he couldn't bring himself to go to her. If Clay had still been at her house, he might not have been able to stop with his nose this time. The anger surrounded him again as he thought of Clay kissing her goodnight. He was the only person to be kissed by those soft, full, pink lips.

His mother walked in and smiled at him. "Good morning. Did you and Ray have a good time last night?"

He nodded his head and cleared his throat. "Yes, we did." He couldn't stand lying to his mother. He got up and set his cup on the counter before she could ask any more questions. He walked outside and headed for the barn. He would go to their house and drown out the questions in his head with work. There was still a lot to do on the house, and he only had a few days left. Even if he didn't find some way to make Ray forgive him, he would still need somewhere to escape his parents.

Jake saddled his horse and headed up to the unfinished house. He thought about what Ray would think if she saw it. Would she like it? Think it was too small, too big? He was not sure, but he guessed she would like it; it wasn't much, but it would be theirs. He suddenly felt sad at the idea of Ray not being with him. All these feelings he was having over their breakup only made him more determined to win her back. He knew if he was persistent, he could convince her to continue with their plan. It was no longer about the land. It was so much more.

He wasn't sure he wanted to know how much more. He rode up to the porch and tied his horse. Walking up on the porch, he picked up his tools; they still had to put the paneling on the walls, finish hanging all the interior doors, paint, and move in the furniture. They still had a long way to go, and the days were flying by. Not only did he have to finish their house but he also had to convince Ray to live in it with him as his bride. With a sigh, he walked inside and got started.

Jake looked at J. W. with a wide grin. "Are you serious? It's finished?"

J. W. grinned back. "Yep, all we have to do is move in the furniture. Everything else is finished."

Jake laughed. "Well, thank goodness. One less thing to worry about. We can have the furniture moved in in no time. Now if it was only as easy to get the bride moved in." Jake sighed and looked back to J. W. "I gave her three days to calm down and come around. I thought she would be up here by now, saying she was sorry and that we could work it out."

J. W. laughed out loud. Jake snapped his head up and glared at him. "And what the hell do you find so funny?"

J.W. held up a finger for Jake to wait while he tried to control his breathing, so he could talk. "Jake, you must be really stupid if you think Rayne Whitmore will come crawling back to you. That girl is even more stubborn than you." And laughing again, he added, "If that is even possible." Jake thought about this for a minute. Had Ray been waiting on him to come to her? Well, if she had, he had totally missed the cue.

Jake spoke to J. W. again. "Do you think she will even listen to me if I try to explain what happened?"

J. W. thought about that for a minute then answered, "Boy, you're running out of time here. The best thing to do would be to make her listen." He didn't give Jake a minute to answer before he went on. "I know it will be like pulling teeth, but you have to ask yourself one question." He paused to let that sink in. "How do you see your life without her?" Jake considered the question and answered in one word: "Boring."

J. W. grinned and said, "Then you do what you have to." Jake smiled and turned for the barn. He had to get the wagon and go into town to pick up the furniture. He might just stop by the Circle W and see what Ray was doing on Friday. He didn't care what she had planned because she would be standing in that church house saying her vows to him. He didn't care if he had to tie her up like a calf to get her there.

He hooked up the horses to the wagon and with a nod to J. W., started toward town. J. W. tipped his hat back at Jake and started laughing again. If he knew Jake, there would be some fireworks at the Circle W real soon. He turned and headed to the barn. He wanted to be saddled up and headed out when the excitement started.

When Jake reached town, he pulled the buggy up in front of Jerry's shop. He and his mother had visited Jerry the day after he and Ray had gotten engaged and ordered the usual furniture—a bed frame, dresser, chest of drawers, two small tables for the sitting room, a dining room table, and four chairs. When he walked in and saw Jerry working on a chest, he was surprised. "You working on an order for someone else?" he asked.

Jerry looked up and smiled. "No, this piece was ordered by your mother. Just two days ago. I'm finishing up with it now. The boys finished your other pieces yesterday. Everything is ready."

Jake thought about what he said. His mother had come back and ordered another piece? Why hadn't she said anything to him about it? Given, he had not been home much the last couple of days because he was trying to finish the house. She could have mentioned it at breakfast. That was about the only meal they sat down for, but she hadn't. "You said my mother requested this piece. What is it?" He walked around the worktable and stood next to Jerry.

"It is what the ladies like to call a hope chest. The way I understand it, they put their wedding dress, dishes, and other special things in it and give it to their children when they get old enough to marry. It is something to be passed on to other generations."

Jake looked at the midsized cedar chest. Jerry had finished sanding it. He had put hinges on the lid and secured it to the top of the bottom box which made the storage compartment of the chest. On the top of the chest, he was carving words. Jake leaned in to look at what they were. In large letters, it read, "Jackson and Rayne Hale." He blinked at the way their names flowed so fluidly along the top of the chest. Jerry had scraped out the carving and burnt it so that the words were black and easy to read. Below their names, Jerry was scraping out a carving of the date, "July 18, 1921," only two days away.

Jake swallowed the lump in his throat. He wanted this to happen. He wanted to marry Ray on Friday. He wanted them to live happily together and have children she could pass the memories of their life on to. He wanted that more than he could have imagined. He turned to look at Jerry. "Good, I'm sure Ray will love it. Thank you, Jerry. You have done beautiful work, as always."

Jerry nodded his thanks. Jake looked down the street at the rest of the shops. He needed to go to Baker's also to make sure the mattress and linens had arrived. He told Jerry to have the boy's load the wagon, and he would be back shortly. Jerry nodded in agreement again.

Jake walked up the dusty street toward Baker's store. He wondered how Mr. Baker would treat him after the way he acted at the dance. He was surprised to see him smiling and waving to him on the porch as he walked up. "Hello, Mr. Baker," he said, trying to judge his face.

Mr. Baker smiled and said, "Well, hello, Jake. How are you today?"

Before Jake could answer, he went on, "You're here for your order, I guess. I've got everything you and your mother ordered. Josh will be glad to load it up for you."

"Thanks, Mr. Baker," Jake said as he walked up on the porch. Mr. Baker was looking at him like he had something else to say. Jake looked up at him, waiting on him to continue.

"Uh, Jake, have you talked to Ray lately?" he asked in a small voice.

Jake looked surprised and said, "Well, no, I haven't. Have you seen her? Has she said something about me?"

Mr. Baker cleared his throat and said, "Well, she came in here this morning. She looked real sad and very tired like she hadn't been sleeping well. I asked her if everything was all right, but she wouldn't answer. She came to pick up her father's feed. Josh loaded it for her, and she told him thank you, but she wouldn't speak much. I'm worried about her."

Jake thought about this for a minute. If Ray was really waiting on him to come to her, then she would be worrying about how he felt. What if she thought that he didn't want anything to do with her anymore? If she had feelings for him, then that would break her heart. He sighed at the pain he could be causing her. He smiled as a plan formed in his mind. He would get everything set up in the house then go get Ray and bring her there. He would show her the work he had done to build them a future and offer to share it with her. Surely she would agree. If she was hurting over him, then she would jump at the chance to make everything right again.

CHAPTER 12

Jake and the boys had just finished moving all the furniture in the house. They had set up the bed and arranged all the furniture that had been bought and the furniture his parents had given him. Jake was a little disappointed that it had taken all of the day and into the night to get it finished. He had planned on going and getting Ray and bringing her here to see the finished house. He had no doubt she was asleep. Would she get mad if he dragged her out of bed? He knew the answer; he smiled as he mounted his horse and headed for Ray's house.

Ray was tossing and turning dreams of Jake spun wildly in her mind. For the last three days, she has had a hard time concentrating on anything. Her father has gotten used to it, but the ranch hands seem to be irritated by it. She has tried to stay focused, but all too often, visions of Jake riding up to her and declaring the feelings of his heart have prevailed. The fact that she has gone to the pond every night since they fought does not help matters either. She felt like she was going crazy.

Ray froze for a second. She thought she had heard a pecking sound. She rose up in her bed to look around the room. It was still dark, not quite morning. Her eyes adjusted quickly to the room around her. She looked toward the window. There was soft moonlight drifting in. She heard the noise again. This time, she knew it was coming from her window. She threw the covers back and walked across the bare floor. When she reached the window, she heard the noise again and realized what it was. Someone was throwing stones at her window.

She raised the window slowly trying to make as little noise as possible. Ray's mouth fell open at the shadow of the tall cowboy standing below her window with a handful of smooth stones. Jake grinned. "Shut your mouth, Ray. It's only me, Jake Hale."

Ray cleared her throat and fought back the rush of nerves that were suddenly clawing up her back. "Jake? What are you doing here? It's the middle of the night."

Jake laughed again. "Well, nothing gets by you. Do you know what Friday is?" He waited for her response anxiously.

"Just any old day. Same as the rest," she replied in a whisper.

Jake smiled. "Well, you can remember our wedding day as any old day if you want, but I'm not going to." He laughed again as Ray's eyes widened, and her mouth fell open.

"Jake, we aren't getting married Friday. I called it off." *Please, Jake, tell me how you really feel!* Her mind was screaming at him to admit that he had feelings for her, but Jake wouldn't budge as usual.

He just stood there with a grin on his face. "Get dressed and come down here. I got something to show you that may change your mind." Ray sighed as she thought about this. Maybe he didn't feel comfortable telling her like this. A girl could hope, right?

Ray dressed in a hurry. She grabbed a shirt and pair of pants and threw them on. She slipped her boots on and with a sigh, left her hair down. She walked slowly down the steps trying to keep from waking up her father. When she opened the front door, the rusted spring screeched. She grimaced and closed it. She turned to walk off the porch and found herself nose to nose with Jake. She jumped and bit her tongue to keep from screaming.

Jake grinned even wider. "Sorry I scared you."

She rolled her eyes and said, "Now what is this about showing me something? It's the middle of the night, Jake. I have a lot to do tomorrow."

"Well, you might just have to change your plans for tomorrow after I show you your surprise."

She shook her head and said, "I doubt that, but okay, go ahead. Where is it?" Jake took her arm and started walking off the porch. When he reached his horse, Ray planted her feet and stopped. "What are you doing? You didn't say anything about leaving. I don't want to leave. Just tell me what you want to tell me."

Jake shook his head. "I want to show you something, and we have to go somewhere else for me to show you. Now stop being stubborn and get on the horse."

"No." Ray shook her head. "I can ride my own horse, thank you. What is so important that it can't wait 'til morning?"

Jake shook his head getting inpatient. Why couldn't the bull-headed woman just get on the horse? Did she plan on making his life hell, or was it just a plus? "Ray, get on the damn horse before I throw you on it myself!" He moved like he was going to grab her, and she instantly became defensive.

"No, Jake! I said I can ride my own horse!"

A grumpy sound coming from the house made Jake laugh and Ray scowl. "Rayne Whitmore, get on the damn horse, or I am going to whoop your butt!" She huffed and climbed on the horse. Jake climbed up behind her and reached around her to pick up the reins. As they rode away, Ray could still hear her father's grumpy outbursts. She laughed to herself trying not to let Jake hear her.

They rode in silence, only the sound of their breathing to keep them company. They passed the pond and started up the hill. Ray had thought he would be taking her to their pond, but now she was really puzzled when he passed it up without a glance. She tried to rack her brain to figure out where they were going. It was the wrong direction for his house. There was nothing but pasture, as far as she knew, in the direction he was heading.

When they reached the top of the hill, the land smoothed out level for a few acres. Ray gasped in shock as her eyes took in the image in front of her. The house was gorgeous. Like a little cabin. It had a wide porch on the front and another, she guessed, on the back. There were two windows in the front and the front door had a red bow tied to it. She couldn't speak; she was still too shocked to form full words.

Jake leaned toward her putting his lips to her ear. "I wanted you to see *our* house." He paused for a few seconds. "I know I screwed this up, but I'm not taking no for an answer. I want you to be my wife."

She turned her face toward him. He buried his in her hair. "Why?" she breathed.

The suspense was killing her. After a few seconds, Jake answered, "Isn't it obvious? Because I can't live without *you* driving me crazy!" He paused again, trying to judge her reaction.

She stayed still, only the quick pace of her heart told him she had heard him. He waited for her response. "What are you saying, Jake?" she whispered softly. She turned herself in the saddle, so she could look into his face.

Jake looked in her eyes. Slowly, he took her face in his hands. Had she not caught what he had said? The doubt he saw in her eyes made him angry. He slipped his hand around the back of her neck and pulled her face to his. His mouth was hard and hot on hers. She closed her eyes and relaxed her mouth under his. God, she was in heaven.

The way she felt when he was holding her, kissing her, could not be matched by anything in the world. She felt like she was flying, soaring above everything. This had to be a dream, but she had never known her imagination to be so vivid. Jake's mouth softened on hers. He slid his tongue along her bottom lip, urging her to open her mouth. She parted her lips, and he slowly slid his tongue into her mouth; a satin touch, warm and wet.

She sighed and pushed herself into his hard chest, wrapping her arms around his neck. She slipped her hand into his hair. Feeling the long strands of his black hair curled around her fingers, she pulled her mouth from his and rested her forehead against his. She softly breathed his name; a whisper between them. "Please tell me this is not a dream." She paused to breath. "I have dreamed of this so much I can't tell if it is real or not." She took another breath. "Please don't let me wake up, Jake. I don't want this to end."

She laid her face into his chest and took a deep breath. He smelled so masculine, like cedar and hay mixed with a sweet smell like flowers. Jake kissed the top of her head and whispered, "Honey, all you have to do is show up at the church tomorrow. I don't care if you're wearing a flour sack for a dress." He laughed to himself and went on. "We will live in this dream for the rest of our lives. You won't ever have to wake up as long as you're with me."

She looked up at him with tears in her eyes. "Jake, are you telling me you love me?" Jake sighed and shook his head yes. "I been trying to tell you I love you since you came down the stairs in that blue dress. I haven't been able to catch my breath since. Please marry me, Ray? I'll beg if I have to."

Ray grinned. "Even though I would love to hear you beg, I will go easy on you." She paused then whispered "yes."

Jake laughed and grabbed her in a bear hug. "Well, it's about damn time!" Ray laughed and hugged him back.

"Jake, I don't want to see the house now. I want it to be a surprise."

Jake nodded in agreement. "Whatever you want. That's fine with me."

Ray turned back around in the saddle. Jake wrapped his arms around her again and picked up the reins. As Jake turned the horse back toward her house, she settled back against him. With a sigh of contentment, she closed her eyes. She was so excited yet also relieved. All those nights sitting by the pond waiting for him to come and declare his love for her; he had been on top of the hill building a house that would bring them back together. Now all she had to do was say "I do" and her dreams would come true.

CHAPTER 13

As morning broke through the window, Ray stretched and breathed a sigh of relief. She and Jake had made up, and he professed his love for her. She could confidently stand and vow to be his wife knowing he loved her. Ray thought about her parents and how much they had loved each other until her mother's dying day. Her father was never interested in another woman. She wondered if that was true love, so strong that after one is gone, you can't bring yourself to love another.

She heard her father walk by the door going downstairs for coffee. She grinned. That was just what she needed to wake her up, a big ole cup of coffee! She hopped out of bed and headed downstairs. She went up to the stove and poured her a cup of the delicious brew. Cupping her hands around the cup, she took a seat at the table.

Her dad took one look at her and started grinning. "Well, I guess you and Jake worked out your differences last night?"

"Yes, we did. Did you know he was building us a house?"

Her dad scratched his chin, "Well, he may have mentioned it. What did you think that the both of you would live here with me or with his parents?"

Sheepishly, she admitted, "I didn't put much thought into it."

"Well, luckily, Jake did. The two of you have to work out how to live together and make decisions. You don't need anyone hanging around for those fights. It's better for it to just be the two of you."

Ray looked sad for a moment and looked to her father. "Dad, I don't know how to be a wife. I can't cook, sew, or wash. What am I supposed to do for a husband?"

With tears in his eyes, her father looked at her. "Rayne, you do what you do best. Be yourself. You are a strong, hardworking, loyal, and loving woman. You will figure it out." He paused for a minute to clear his throat. "Don't give up on this boy when he does something you don't like. You stay and fight it out. Don't ever walk away, and he will never walk away from you."

As the tears fell down her cheeks, she nodded her head. "I will, Daddy." She sniffed and wiped her nose. As Emma came through the back door, Ray stood up and finished her coffee. "Well, let's get this started then." Just as they were going to head up stairs, there was a knock on the front door. Ray passed through the living room and pulled open the door. Sarah Hale stood on the porch holding an envelope. "Good morning," she offered.

"Morning," Ray returned with a look of curiosity. "Is everything okay with Jake?" Sensing the curiosity and slight anxiety in Ray's tone, Jake's mother assured her, "Yes, dear, everything is fine. I thought I would come and help you get ready if that's all right?"

Ray grinned. "Yes, that would be nice." She opened the door and moved back, so Sarah could enter. Sarah smiled to Ray's father, and they all headed upstairs. Once in Ray's room, Sarah moved to the closed door where the dress bag hung. "I hope it looks okay on me. I haven't seen it since I was measured."

Sarah smiled. "I am sure it will be perfect." Emma excused herself to draw Ray a bath. Once they were alone, Sarah handed the envelope to Ray. "It is from Jake. I advised him to write what he was feeling since he sometimes struggles with telling someone. He surprised me by actually doing it. I will check on Emma while you read it."

Ray slowly opened the envelope and drew out the paper. She took a deep breath and started reading.

Ray,

My mother told me sometimes it was easier to write what you feel instead of saying it. She was right. I am sorry for the way I have treated you. I did not realize how it was hurting you.

I teased you so much when we were kids 'cause you were always so good at stuff, and I couldn't stand to be outdone by a girl.

I am okay with it now. It may take a little while to get used to being a husband. I hope I don't let you down.

When I do something wrong, please forgive me.

See you soon.

Love,
Jake

Wiping tears from her eyes, she hugged the letter to her and prayed that she would be strong enough to stand up in front of everyone and pledge her heart to Jake. She was so nervous and scared. Taking a deep breath, she laid the letter on the bedside table and headed to get a bath.

CHAPTER 14

Ray stood back and looked to Emma and then Sarah. She had lost her breath when she saw the dress. Now that she had it on, she wondered if it would still be as beautiful. Emma and Sarah both were wiping tears from their eyes. Ray spun around laughing, raising her hands in the air. Emma and Sarah joined her laughing and clapping at her happy spirit. "Ray," Sarah broke in, "you are so very beautiful. Your mother would be so proud." Ray stopped laughing and took a silent moment to think of her mother. How wonderful it would be to have her by her side, helping her get ready for her wedding, but it wasn't meant to be. She knew without a doubt that her mother would be smiling down on her today.

"Well, it's time," Sarah's quiet voice broke into Ray's thoughts. She gathered her overnight bag and got ready to go downstairs. Emma and Sarah went on downstairs as Ray took one last look at her room. So many memories in this house. She was excited to start this new chapter in her life but also a little sad to be leaving the only home she had ever known.

As she made her way downstairs, her father had cleaned up and changed. He was standing at the foot of the stairs wearing clean jeans, a white shirt, and a black jacket. Smiling widely, she reached him and wrapped him in a hug. "My sweet little girl." He spoke softly. "You are a beautiful young lady, and Jake is very lucky to have you as his wife." He sniffed back tears and stepped back. "I have something for you." Reaching into his pocket, he pulled out a little box. "I gave these to your mother on our wedding day." Opening the box, it was a beautiful pearl necklace. "It is only right for you to have them on your wedding day." She held back the tears as he turned her around and fastened the pearls around her neck.

"Thank you, Daddy," she choked out.

Clearing his throat, her father announced, "Well, let's not keep this boy waiting." They all walked outside to the buggy that was waiting. Ray sat close to the window looking out at the sky full of clouds and wondering how Jake would react when he saw her. Would he smile or look bewildered? She could only guess as they got closer to the church. The butterflies were working overtime in her stomach as the time for her to walk down the aisle grew closer.

CHAPTER 15

Jake paced back-and-forth in the Sunday school room. *How much longer?* He looked at his pocket watch for the fifteenth time. His father stepped in and asked if he was ready. "You bet!" He followed him out to the sanctuary, taking his place to the right of the preacher. The preacher gave him a welcoming smile, and the piano started up. Looking to the double doors at the front of the church, he waited patiently for his bride to step through.

The doors were pushed open, and the foyer was empty. Seconds seemed like minutes before she stepped into view. Rayne was a vision in a white lace dress. The sleeves reached all the way to her fingers and down to the tops of her shoes. White lace brushed the tops of her breasts. She was gorgeous. He stood very still with a small smile on his face. Her red hair was curled and pulled back loosely to let some curls escape to touch her neck and shoulders. She was clutching a bouquet of white flowers and walking with her father very slowly toward him. His eyes locked with hers, and for a moment, it was only the two of them in the church.

Her father cleared his throat to get Jake's attention. He looked to her father with wide eyes. "Her mother and I," her father stated and placed Ray's hand in Jake's. He looked down at their connected hands and grinned. It was actually happening. She stepped up beside him and turned to face him. As the preacher began to speak, he kept his eyes locked on Ray's. He could see nervousness and curiosity in her eyes. He tried his best to convey his love to her. The last thing he wanted was her to feel alone or afraid on their wedding day. The preacher finished and looked to Jake to recite his vows. He repeated the preacher's words loud and clear, hoping she would see how serious he was about being her husband. Her turn came, and she shakily put the ring on his finger and repeated her vows. He smiled softly at her as she tried to remember all the words. She gave a sigh of relief when she finished.

Soon enough, the preacher was pronouncing them husband and wife and telling Jake to kiss his bride. He moved in and wrapped an arm around her. Taking his time, he slowly pulled her into him. As soft as he could, he pressed his lips to hers and sealed their bond. With cheers from the crowd, they embraced a second time grinning at each other.

They headed out of the church down the steps to the buggy as rice and shouts of congratulations followed them. Jake helped her in the buggy and then took his place beside her. Picking up the reins, he set the team to a walk as Ray threw her bouquet out the window.

They rode in silence for a while until Jake finally got up the courage to tell her how beautiful she looked. She thanked him shyly but remained quiet. As they pulled up in front of their house, he slowed the wagon and jumped down to tie off the team. Coming around the buggy, he moved to help her down, but she quickly jumped out before he could touch her. He grabbed the bags and took them to the porch. She came up the steps and met him at the front door. He opened the door and quickly scooped her up before she could protest. Carrying her across the threshold, he announced, "Welcome home, Mrs. Hale."

Breathless and laughing, she kicked her feet expecting him to put her down. Her heart did double time as he kept walking with her in his arms to the bedroom. He slowly put her down beside the bed. She couldn't look at him; she was too nervous. Turning away from him, she spoke softly. "I need just a moment." He stood still, looking at her.

He came up behind her and spoke softly in her ear. "Sweetheart, you can take all the time you need. I know this is scary, but it's going to be okay. I won't hurt you."

She breathed a sigh of relief and leaned back against him. He wrapped his arms around her and held her tight. Kissing the top of her head, he told her, "I need to go unhook the buggy and put the horses up."

"Okay," she said and held onto his hand as he walked toward the door.

Once he was outside, she berated herself. You are a strong woman who can do the work of two men, and you cower at making love to your husband? How hard can it be! She started to remove her dress but was having trouble getting to all the buttons. She huffed and grabbed her bag. She quickly started putting her clothes into the wardrobe, smiling to herself when she saw that Jake's were already there. Once she finished unpacking her bag, she walked through the house looking at the living room first and then the kitchen. She was studying the stove when Jake walked back in. He stopped and looked at her staring at the stove. He smiled to himself; she was the cutest thing.

She jumped slightly when he came up behind her wrapping an arm around her stomach. Drawing her to him, he kissed her neck behind her ear and heard her sharp intake of breath. "What are you thinking?" she wondered for a minute if she should tell him and finally spoke. "I am wondering how long it will take us to starve."

He laughed out loud. "Don't you worry about that. I forgot to show you something." He walked her to the back of the house, and a hundred feet from the door was another small house. It looked only big enough for a living room and bedroom.

"Don't worry about cooking," Jake said softly. "You can go into town and recruit us some help. You will be busy helping me set out the new fencing and rounding up the herd. Unless you object, that is."

She shook her head. "No, I do not object. I want to learn to cook, but I need something to do in the meantime." She turned and took his face in her hands. Kissing him softly, she pushed her hands up into his hair. He pulled her into him as close as they could get. She pulled back and asked softly, "Could you help me with something important?"

He replied, "Of course, anything you need."

She smiled softly and took his hand leading him back toward the bedroom. "I can't seem to get these pesky buttons undone. I was hoping my husband could help me get out of this dress."

Jake grinned. "Well, you sure picked the right person to help. I am working on becoming an expert at getting you naked!"

She laughed and pulled him into the bedroom, shutting the door behind them.

The End

About the Author

M. J. Carley resides in rural Alabama with her motorcycle-riding hubby and unruly teenage boys; she has frequent adventures with her friends and loves spending hours on end at the lake house with her family. Her love of reading and wild imagination helps her to craft fantastic tales of drama, love, and laughter.

CPSIA information can be obtained
at www.ICGtesting.com
Printed in the USA
LVHW030026120720
660355LV00002B/254